DREAM

NEW YORK TIMES BESTSELLING AUTHOR

Carly Phillips

Copyright © Karen Drogin, CP Publishing 2018
Print Edition
Cover Photo: Sara Eirew
Cover Design: Melissa Gill Designs

* * *

This book is a work of fiction. Names, characters, places, and incidents either are
products of the author's imagination or are used fictitiously. Any resemblance to
actual events or locales or persons, living or dead, is entirely coincidental.

She was his best friend, his first love. And she broke his heart. Now she's back. Will they find a second chance?

As a little girl, Andrea Harmon wanted to marry a prince, and Kyle Davenport hoped it would be him. But he never told her how he felt, and lost her as a result. Because sometimes the bad guy gets the girl. And Kyle left town to get over her.

Andi made the wrong choice years ago, choosing the bad boy over the best friend she trusted and she paid for it every day since.

Coming face to face with his former best friend was bound to happen once he moved back to Rosewood Bay, but for Kyle, becoming her son's new teacher is a painful reminder of what they never had. But this time around, Kyle is determined to change their ending. Prince Charming is determined to break down her walls.

Except that no happily-ever-after is won without a fight – and her ex-husband doesn't like to lose.

Chapter One

ANDI HARMON ENJOYED afternoon parties, as they were rare in her life. As a single mom, full-time manager of the town's floral shop, In Bloom, and exhausted human being, she didn't get out much for fun. Her brother, Kane, and his wife, Halley, who'd just announced her pregnancy, were hosting the event for Halley's recently found sister. And since they lived on the beach, Andi now stood overlooking the gorgeous bay, talking to Phoebe, another of Halley's sisters, and Juliette, the guest of honor.

She glanced out to where the boys, her eight-year-old son, Nicky, and Phoebe's thirteen-year-old son, Jamie, were down by the water. She kept an eye on the kids as she talked to Phoebe about their upcoming school year. Juliette, who was new to town and didn't have any children, just listened.

"So I hear there's a new teacher for Nicky's grade," Phoebe was saying.

Andi had known the district would need to replace Mrs. Briggs, who was pregnant and had given notice that she wouldn't be returning, but Andi had been out of the loop regarding a replacement. As a small district, they only had one teacher per grade.

"His name is Mr. Davenport," Phoebe continued.

Andi's heart stopped at the last name. "*Kyle* Davenport?" she asked, her heart in her throat.

"As a matter of fact, yes." Phoebe looked at her with a curious expression. "Do you know him?"

"From a long time ago," she murmured, unwilling to put something extremely personal out for discussion. She was a private person, had learned to be out of necessity.

The last time she'd seen or spoken to Kyle had been to ask him to go away, to leave her alone and not bother her ever again. Her heart squeezed at the memory of how she'd turned her back on her best friend. And though she'd had the purest reasons in the world and had only been protecting him, he hadn't known that. He'd just been aware of her rejection.

"Well, I hear he's hot," Phoebe said, unaware that the more she spoke about Kyle Davenport, the more uncomfortable Andi became.

Phoebe nudged Andi with her elbow. "You never know. He could be the right guy for you."

If only Phoebe knew the truth. Kyle had been her everything, from the time they were young until she'd gone and become infatuated with Billy Gray, high school quarterback and the guy every girl wanted to date. *Be careful what you wish for*, she thought now, because she'd caught Billy's attention, and nothing had ever been the same.

She wrapped her arms around herself, suddenly chilled despite the warm day. "I don't date," she said, wanting this conversation to end. "I'm too busy with Nicky and work."

Juliette frowned at her abrupt comment, as did Phoebe.

"And you know I think that's a crock," Phoebe said. "You're gorgeous and have a great personality. You could get any guy you wanted and he'd be lucky to have you."

"Why don't we talk about something else," Juliette suggested, obviously catching on to Andi's discomfort. "Is Jamie excited about going back to school?" she asked Phoebe.

"He wants to see his friends. Schoolwork? Not so much." Phoebe laughed. "Typical, I guess."

Shaken by the news that Kyle was not only back in town but would be her son's teacher, Andi stopped listening to the conversation. She needed a few minutes alone to process and pull herself together.

"Excuse me," she murmured and walked to the far side of the back porch and leaned against the railing, breathing in the fresh salt air and exhaling again.

Kyle had become a teacher? She sifted through

3

what she remembered about him in her mind. A lover of books, good with his younger brother, and kind… Yes, she could see him becoming an educator, working with kids. The times she'd run into his mother, they'd avoided talking about Kyle. Though it had been unspoken, his mom understood that the issues and the pain ran deep. But whatever she knew about what had happened between them, she'd always been kind to Andi through the years.

Now she had to come face-to-face with her past and the lies she'd told. She wouldn't blame Kyle if he still hated her for being so cruel to him not long after graduation. As much as she'd like to make things right now, to explain why she'd turned him away, that would be admitting how weak she'd been when it came to Billy, the horrible things she'd put up with while married to him.

And those were secrets she never planned to reveal.

KYLE DAVENPORT WAITED for Nicky's mother to arrive for his requested meeting after the school day ended. He sat at his desk looking over his students' work, his gaze unfocused on the papers he'd have to grade tonight because right now his thoughts kept drifting to the past.

His past with Andi Harmon. When he'd received the class list and then the parents filled out and sent back the emergency forms, Kyle had been struck by the fact that although her son's name was Nicky *Gray*, Andi had changed her name back to Harmon after the divorce. A divorce he'd only found out about after moving back to Rosewood Bay at the end of the summer. His mother knew better than to discuss Andi with him, so he hadn't kept up on her life. He hadn't wanted to know.

When Kyle decided to return home, it had been an easy decision, at least as far as his family was concerned. What was harder was knowing he'd have to see Andi again. He'd left after high school graduation, going to college and then graduate school for his master's in education, coming home only for holidays and visits but settling in Illinois and teaching there.

But his mother had fallen this past spring and broken her hip, and he'd been stuck in another state, teaching there, unable to be around to help. He'd known then, he'd be coming home to Connecticut for good as soon as his current school year ended.

He was the first to admit his years away had been him running away. Andi's harsh rejection had stung almost as badly as her choosing to date the high school quarterback and guy with the bad reputation despite Kyle's warning her not to. It wasn't so much that he hated the man she'd ultimately decided to date then marry – though he did – but he'd still tried to respect his best friend's choice.

It was, however, the fact that she'd turned her back on their lifelong friendship and never looked back that still burned in his gut. His ego had taken a hit, yes, but so had his heart. Because though they'd been best friends, he'd always loved her. He just hadn't had the courage to act on his feelings, and by the time he'd been ready to, she'd captured Billy Gray's attention and Kyle had lost his opportunity. Eventually he'd lost Andi.

But he was back now and he had to deal with her in order to help her son, who, he'd noticed immediately, had reading and comprehension issues compared to the other kids in his grade. He never liked having to give parents news that would throw them, but there were so many ways to help a smart boy like Nicky overcome problems.

He turned his attention back to the papers on his desk, still not seeing them clearly, while he waited for her arrival, but he couldn't stop thinking about Andi and what she was like now. How the years had changed her. How her marriage to that asshole had further altered her sweet, good-natured personality, because the woman who'd abandoned their friendship hadn't been the Andi he knew.

A knock sounded and he glanced up to find her waiting in the doorframe. She wore a pair of dark jeans and a purple blouse, her wavy brown hair tumbling over her shoulders, her brown eyes wide and wary in her pretty face.

Looking at her up close was like a punch in the gut. She'd grown into her potential as a woman, her natural beauty shining through, from the dusting of freckles on her nose to the hint of cleavage exposed where her soft shirt dipped lightly in front, revealing a hint of a lace bra and generous breasts.

He rose to his feet. "Come on in," he said in a gruff voice, pissed off at himself for noticing her attributes.

She stepped inside and walked over to his desk. "Hi," she said, her tone soft.

"Hi."

An awkward silence followed. Since introductions weren't necessary and any *how have you been* conversation would only be awkward and disingenuous, he figured he'd get right to the point, but before he could gather his thoughts, she spoke.

"How have you been?" she asked.

He shot her a sharp look. They weren't here for catching up. "Why don't we sit down and discuss the reason you're here."

She jerked at his abrupt tone and obvious dismissal

of small talk, but she pulled herself together quickly. "Is everything okay with Nicky?" she asked, her tone betraying her genuine concern for her son.

"Have a seat." He gestured to the chair in front of the metal desk.

She did as he asked, crossing her long legs and leaning forward, obviously open to whatever he was going to tell her. He appreciated that she didn't automatically get defensive and assume the worst like some parents did. A responsive parent made his job easier. And if he was going to deal with Andi despite their pasts, he needed her open to his thoughts.

"I realize we're only a few weeks into the school year, but I've noticed some behaviors in Nicky that indicate to me he has an issue with reading," he said, not beating around the bush.

Her eyes opened wide. "I know he has trouble reading but I thought he was just a slow learner. You know, like it was a boy thing."

Kyle shook his head. "He struggles to recognize words that are grade appropriate and he avoids reading out loud when asked." He went on to explain other behaviors he'd noticed.

She glanced down at her hands, wringing them together. "He told me he feels dumb when he's reading but I just thought that was his frustration talking." She dabbed at her eyes, obviously upset she'd missed that something was wrong. "I should have paid more attention. The days are just so busy, between work and school, homework and afterschool activities."

He didn't want to feel bad for her, dammit. But he was affected by her emotions anyway, despite his not wanting to get personally involved with her problems. He wanted to help her child, nothing more, nothing less.

He rose from his seat and walked around the desk, sitting in a chair beside her. Her peach scent immediately drifted toward him and affected him on a primal level. He'd hoped – hell, he'd spent nights praying – that the desire he'd felt for her years ago had disappeared. That in the decade or so that had passed, he'd gotten over her. From the way he admired her looks to the fact that his heart squeezed at her obvious pain for her son, that hadn't happened.

He ignored the purely biological reaction and pushed aside the emotional one, focusing on the reason for the meeting instead. It was normal for parents to blame themselves for not catching a problem with their child, but the truth was, the days did pass quickly, and as a teacher, he had Nicky for more hours of the day than she did.

He reached out to touch her hand, then reflexively pulled back, not wanting to cross a personal barrier. If he wouldn't do it with any other parent, he sure as hell wasn't about to with Andi. "It's not your job to know what's age and grade appropriate. It's mine. And there's good news in this, too."

"What?" she asked, looking up at him with hopeful brown eyes.

He cleared his throat. "We're a small class and it's easy for me to make accommodations. I was trained in language-based difficulties. I can do some work after class and help him gain strategies to make things easier for him."

"You'd do that?" she asked, obviously surprised he'd put himself out for her.

"It's my job."

She swallowed hard and nodded, glancing away. "Right. So what can I do at home to help him?"

He couldn't deny that she was obviously a good, caring mother. "Encourage him," he said. "Verbally reward his effort, not just the end result, and most of all, be patient with him. Don't let him feel your stress or anxiety over the situation. We want him engaged during the process."

Rising to his feet, he effectively ended the meeting. She caught on and stood, too. "Thank you for catching this."

He nodded. "If Nicky seems overly stressed by things, we can bring in the school psychologist, but if he doesn't mind the extra help after school, let's start there."

She gathered her purse and met his gaze. "I appreciate you not making this meeting awkward." She treated him to a hesitant smile. "Since Nicky's in your class and now you're working with him, we're going to need to put our past aside… for his sake."

"I'm a professional, Andi. My students come before any personal issues I might have." In other words, he still held a grudge for how she'd treated him all those years ago and he didn't want her to think otherwise.

It wasn't easy dealing with her now, still as beautiful as she'd always been and just as elusive to him as ever.

ANDI WALKED OUT of Kyle's classroom, holding on to her last shred of dignity and composure. Only once she was certain he'd shut the door behind her did she lean against the nearest wall, allowing it to hold her up as she pulled herself together.

She didn't know what she'd expected he would look like now, but he'd changed… and yet he'd stayed the same. His hair was still a dark brown, caught beneath the fluorescent lights, and fell over his forehead in a way that was so familiar it made her throat swell. He wore a light blue button-down shirt, sleeves rolled up, revealing tanned forearms with muscles he hadn't possessed before that made her wonder what his chest looked like underneath. His jeans molded to strong thighs and a sexy ass.

She'd never looked at him as a sexy man before and the revelation was as startling as it was confusing. He'd been her best friend and now she saw *him*. All of him. Including the cool expression on his face and in his golden-brown eyes when he looked at her. And refused to exchange the most basic of pleasantries.

She should have expected it but she hadn't had to consider how he'd treat her. Until now, Kyle Davenport had been Nicky's phantom teacher. She hadn't had to deal with him directly. She had, however, been subjected to her son extolling his virtues over and over again. Mr. Davenport was Nicky's favorite teacher *ever*. Bar none.

Knowing she was going to see him, her stomach had been in knots all day as she'd worked, and since Hannah, her part-time girl, had called in sick, Andi hadn't had time to go home and freshen up before going to talk to Kyle. She'd just shown up and hoped for the best.

So many years had passed, but when she looked at him, she couldn't help feeling like it was just yesterday they'd been together, best pals, unable to conceive of anything coming between them.

But something – someone – had. She had to accept that he'd never treat her the same way again.

She stood up, straightened her shoulders, and strode out of the school, reminding herself her priority wasn't her nonexistent relationship with Kyle. Her most important concern was her son and she'd do anything to make learning easier for him.

She stopped at the supermarket and shopped for ingredients to make dinner before heading to her brother's garage to pick up Nicky where he'd gone after school. He liked to hang out with his uncle Kane and his grandpa, and when Kane was busy, her father tried to keep Nicky occupied with his homework and help Andi out at the same time.

She walked into the front offices to find her son sitting across from her father at the desk, holding a handful of cards in his hand.

She cleared her throat.

Her father, Jonathan, jumped. "No betting going on, I swear," he said before Andi could ask or, better yet, accuse.

Her father was a gambler at heart, having never been able to give up any game he thought he could win. The problem was, he thought he could win them all, usually lost, and ended up deep in debt. After his last escapade, Andi had moved out of her father's house, she and Nicky finding their own place.

She was lucky. An older couple, looking to keep their home, had leased their house to Andi. She had a beautiful place to live and she didn't have to worry whether her father was out all night or taking money she left lying around.

"Mom!" Nicky tossed the cards on the table and rose from his seat. Her boy had grown so much, he was tall and lanky, long arms and legs, with her dark brown hair. There wasn't much of his father in him, not in looks and definitely not in bullying personality, and she'd always been glad about that.

"Hi, Nicky. Hi, Dad." She smiled at them both, unwilling to get into an argument with her father over the cards.

"What did Mr. Davenport want to meet about?" Nicky asked.

She reached out to ruffle the top of his head, then thought better of it. He was getting too old for her spontaneous, baby-like touches, as he called them. He'd always be her baby, not that he wanted to hear that.

"Mr. Davenport wanted to talk about your reading," she said carefully.

"Ugh. I hate it," he muttered.

"And he thinks he knows why. Let's talk about it over dinner, but just know Kyle – I mean Mr. Davenport – thinks he can help you feel better about it." She smiled at him in reassurance. "Are you ready to go home?"

"He finished his homework," her dad said.

"Great! So you'll have free time," she told Nicky. "Ready to go?"

"Hi, sis!" Kane joined them, wiping his hand on a rag as he entered from the garage. He'd been her rock for as long as she'd let him be.

"Hi! How are you?" she asked.

"Couldn't be better. About to go home to my wife."

Andi rolled her eyes playfully. Her brother and his wife were all about PDA and she was happy for them. Growing up, Halley's life hadn't been easy, and it had taken meeting and falling in love with Kane for her to open up to people in general. And her brother had finally found the right woman for him. She wasn't jealous. She'd accepted the fact that she'd made some very wrong choices in her life and was just grateful that Billy had found another woman to focus on and no longer cared about his family at all.

He'd met a wealthy woman who had been vacationing in Rosewood Bay for the summer, someone who could finance his spending. He'd been only too happy to give Andi full custody of Nicky and relinquish all responsibilities in life. She was spared from his domineering ways and his temper and that's all she cared about.

She wasn't interested in another man taking control of her life in any way.

Because Andi worked during the day and couldn't be at school to volunteer, she liked to participate in evening PTA events. At least then, Nicky would still know she was interested in what was important to him. Tonight was an ice cream social to bring the kids together for a fun night and raise money for a new school playground at the same time.

She changed into a pair of jeans and a white tee shirt, and she and Nicky arrived at the school gym early to help with the setup. Her friend Georgia Hannity greeted her in front of the ice cream table. Vanilla, chocolate, and strawberry tubs sat on the table ready to be served to the kids.

Georgia was the head of the PTA and a genuinely warm person. Added to that, with her blonde hair and blue eyes, she was gorgeous. She was easy to like.

"Hey!" Georgia pulled her into a hug. "It's good to see you."

Andi smiled. "It's good to see you, too."

"Where's Mark?" Nicky asked of his friend who was the same age.

"He's helping his dad hang streamers." Georgia

pointed to the back of the room, where her husband, Rick, stood on a ladder, attaching paper streamers and curling them and taping them to the wall.

"You are lucky to have a man who helps not only around the house but around school," Andi said with a smile as Nicky ran off to see his friend.

"He's a keeper," Georgia agreed. "Speaking of keepers, have you seen the kids' teacher?" She fanned herself with her hand. "Mr. Davenport is hot."

A slow flush crawled up Andi's face at the mention of Kyle's name. "He's good-looking," she agreed. And that was putting it mildly.

Georgia leaned in close. "Rumor has it he's single."

"He is. And I grew up with him," Andi admitted, because Georgia and her husband were recent transplants to Rosewood Bay and hadn't gone to school with them back in the day.

"So you're friends? Or more? Because you should know every single mom is interested in getting to know him, in the Biblical sense." Georgia had always been a direct, get-right-to-the-point kind of woman.

Jealousy trickled through her at the thought of him with other women, which was ridiculous considering the nonexistent state of their relationship and the fact that, other than their one meeting, she hadn't seen him in years.

She really didn't want to talk about Kyle. She

wanted to talk about Kyle and her even less. "How have you been?" she asked her friend, changing the subject.

"Fine if you count the stomach virus that went through our house last week." Georgia made an ugh face followed by a gagging sound.

Andi nodded in understanding. "Nicky came down with it, gave it to me, and I missed two days of work."

"But we're all healthy now, right?"

Andi held up a hand and crossed her fingers. "Here's hoping it stays that way." Every parent walking into the room could relate to that, she thought. "What can I do to help?"

Georgia glanced around the room. "Care to scoop ice cream?" she finally asked.

"Whatever you need." Andi positioned herself behind the table and picked up a scooper.

Soon after, Georgia announced the ice cream station was open and the line began to form. Andi worked for thirty minutes, digging the metal scooper into the hard ice cream and serving the kids, until someone came by to take over. Her hands were sticky and cold, her shirt covered in stains, but the children were high on sugar and happy, which all that mattered.

She headed to the bathroom to wash up, weaving her way through the kids who had drifted into the hall.

One look at the line outside the kids' lavatory and the memory of the tiny bathrooms had her detouring to the ladies' adult lounge near the main office, where she could have privacy and five minutes of quiet before she returned to the gym.

Once in the bathroom, she washed her hands with soapy water, removing the sticky ice cream. Though her shirt needed a good cleaning, there was nothing she could do about it now. She dried her hands and walked out of the women's lounge, bumping into a hard male body.

"Whoa," a familiar voice said, grasping her forearms at the same time.

"I'm so sorry." She grabbed on to Kyle to steady herself, her hands holding on to firm muscles that flexed beneath her palms.

He smelled of a woodsy cologne that assaulted her senses and made her hyperaware of him as a desirable man, and it had been a long time since that had happened.

She immediately released him, stepping back. "I didn't think anyone else was on this side of the school."

"I had to grab something from my classroom."

"Are you here for the ice cream social?" she asked.

He nodded. "I promised the kids I would stop by."

She couldn't help but smile at his dedication. "I

know Nicky will be thrilled to see you. You're his favorite teacher."

"That's good to know." An adorable dimple appeared in one cheek as he held back a grin. "Looks like you've been working hard," he said, his gaze falling to her chocolate- and strawberry-stained tee shirt, her nipples immediately hardening beneath his gaze and, she realized as she glanced down, totally visible thanks to her white tee shirt.

She met his gaze, her face on fire, just as he reached out to touch her and then drew his hand back and frowned.

"Ready to go back to the gym?" he asked, voice curt, obviously not pleased with himself for noticing her in *that* way. He clearly didn't want to spend any more time talking to her.

But considering her son was in his class and they were bound to randomly run into each other, she didn't want to let him make things awkward between them.

"Before we go, I have something I want to tell you," she said.

"About Nicky?"

She shook her head. "No. About us."

"There's nothing to say." He turned to walk away and she grasped his arm, unprepared for the rush of heat she experienced from touching him again.

"It's going to be a long year if we can't get beyond the past."

His scowl was distinctly unfriendly. "What do you want, Andi? To exchange confidences and be best friends again? You made damned sure that's not going to happen. *Go away and don't call me again* was pretty clear, even over a decade later."

She winced at the memory. Billy had been standing by her side when she'd called Kyle, his hand on her arm, the subtle twist of pain making it all too clear what he'd do to her and to Kyle if she didn't end the friendship and sever their close connection.

"But you're right," he said before she could come up with a reply. "We have to deal with each other and the least I can do is be civil. How is Nicky dealing with our meetings after school? Does he feel singled out?" he asked, sounding concerned when it came to her son.

It wasn't the friendship they'd once had, but he was back to being nice and she'd take it as a baby step.

"He actually likes the attention. I think knowing he's doing something to tackle the reading problem is helping him emotionally, too."

"Good. That's one hurdle down."

"It is," she agreed. "How do you like teaching here?" she asked.

A slow smile spread across his face, the first genuine one she'd seen from him, and it highlighted how good-looking he was. Sexy, with those golden-brown eyes and chiseled features.

"I love it. The kids are great, I'm back by the beach, and my family is nearby. I really can't ask for more."

"I'm glad," she murmured. She'd gotten what she wanted, a return to a peaceful conversation. She wouldn't push for more. "And now we can walk back to the gym."

Without waiting for an answer, she started walking down the hall. He immediately caught up with her, matching her stride. "How have you been?" he asked, almost begrudgingly.

She smiled a little inside. "Good. Very busy. I used to work two jobs, the flower shop and as a hostess at the Blue Wall, but I got a promotion at the day job, which enabled me to quit and be home weekend nights for Nicky. That was about a year ago. Things have settled down since then. It's all good." Without major stress, since her ex no longer lived in town and all she had to worry about was normal, day-to-day living.

They reached the hallway outside the gym, where a parent was shouting for the kids to get back inside the main room. Kyle immediately stepped up to help herd the children and they responded to him, shuffling inside.

Nicky ran up to her and Kyle was already long gone, talking to a woman who stood way too close for her to be a colleague. Andi ignored the pinch of jealousy she felt watching another female paying attention to Kyle. She didn't have a hold on him. Didn't want one, she reminded herself.

But she was also very aware that he was the first man she'd had any kind of physical or emotional response to in what felt like forever, and that made her nervous. Because she'd promised herself after Billy left that she wouldn't fall for another guy's good looks and charm – even if that man had once been her best friend.

Chapter Two

KYLE GAVE A lot of thought to what Andi had said about them treating each other civilly and with respect. Total forgiveness was a long way off, but he could drop the attitude when they were together. Which made it a lot easier when, for his mother's birthday, he stopped by the flower shop during his lunch hour to order a bouquet for his mom for her birthday.

He walked in, taking in the plants hanging from the ceiling and the colorful flowers set up around the shop. He didn't immediately see anyone in the store, until he looked left and caught sight of Andi standing on a ladder, watering a hanging plant. She wore a pair of tight jeans that molded to her long legs and sexy ass, drawing and keeping his attention there.

He gritted his teeth, reminding himself being civil didn't include being attracted to her, and called out. "Hi!"

She turned, holding on to the sides of the ladder. "Oh! Hello." She carefully climbed down, putting the watering can aside on the counter. "What brings you by?" she asked, greeting him with a smile.

"It's my mom's birthday. I wanted to send a bouquet of flowers."

"Oh, that's nice. How is she doing?"

"She's good. She healed nicely from her fall," he said.

She leaned forward on the counter. "I was sorry to hear about her accident. I'm glad she's better. She must be thrilled to have you back home."

He met her gaze, realizing that, yeah, he could do civil. It wasn't as difficult as he had thought.

And he couldn't help but smile at the memory of his mother's reaction to his phone call that he was moving back. She'd screamed loud enough to pierce his eardrum and yelled for his father to pick up the phone. "I'd say it made her year."

"I always liked your mom," Andi said. "And she's always been sweet to me every time we run into each other."

Ever since they were kids, his mother always had a soft spot for Andi, who'd lost her mom to ovarian cancer when she was seventeen, though she'd been sick long before that. Kyle's mom had been like a second mother to her, stepping up when her mom was too sick to do things. And though he and Andi had parted ways, he'd never given his mother the details as to why they were no longer friends, not wanting to interfere in their relationship.

"What are her favorite colors?" she asked.

"She loves everything bright and cheerful."

"I can arrange something she'll love. No worries. Would you like them delivered or will you pick them up?"

"Delivery is fine… if you deliver on Saturdays?"

"Shouldn't be a problem. My delivery boy is scheduled to work." She pulled out an order form and handwrote the information, including his mother's address for delivery.

He reached into his pocket and pulled out his wallet, removing his credit card, and while she rang up the sale, he handwrote the card, signing it from him and his brother. After she input the information and charged him, he signed and finished the transaction.

"How did you end up working here?" he asked, continuing on in the friendly vein. She'd mentioned once holding down two jobs, which couldn't have been easy for her while raising Nicky. He figured her family must have pitched in a lot to help her out.

She paused before handing him his receipt. "I didn't work when I was married. Billy didn't like– He wanted his wife at home."

He frowned at her admission but he wasn't surprised. Billy had always been a possessive son of a bitch. Kyle had seen much less of Andi once she started seeing the jock football player.

"After he left, I needed a job and Wendy Orr, the owner, needed an employee." She shrugged at the simplicity of the answer. "It was minimum wage but it was work. I certainly didn't have experience or credentials for anything else. And like I mentioned, I used to be a hostess at the Blue Wall on the weekends."

"That must have been hard, holding down two jobs."

She nodded. "It was. But Kane was a great babysitter. My dad, too. You do what you have to do to get by."

He heard the tiredness in her voice, and the notion that she was worn down by life hit him hard, though he admired her work ethic and dedication to her son, something her ex-husband obviously didn't share. Given Billy's controlling nature, Kyle was surprised the man had bailed on his family. Then again, he'd always been lazy and maybe commitment and responsibility had been too much for him. He'd left Andi to work two jobs and raise his child. Stupid, selfish bastard.

"Nicky is lucky to have you," he said.

Her eyes lit up at the mention of her son. "There's nothing I wouldn't do for him."

And that was her most redeeming quality, he thought. He knew what it was like to have a loving mother and had seen the results of children who hadn't been as fortunate. Despite coming from a broken home, Nicky wouldn't fall through the cracks.

Someone walked into the shop, making him realize they'd been having a personal, revealing conversation. Two old friends catching up and it surprised him how much he liked it.

"I should get going." He rapped his knuckles on the counter. "Thanks for the flowers."

"You're welcome. And Kyle, talking to you was… nice."

He inclined his head, unable to deny that it had been.

ANDI WATCHED KYLE leave, her gaze on his sexy ass in his tailored pants, shocked that she was even noticing such a thing. Even more surprised she hadn't been able to take her gaze off where a lock of his hair fell across his forehead as he talked to her, her fingers itching to sweep it back. Was his hair as soft as it looked? And why was she wondering? What was going on with her?

"Hello, Andrea."

Andi blinked at the sound of her name and turned to the next customer, Edna Martin, a sweet older woman who came in weekly for flowers to put on her beloved husband's grave. Andi already knew Mrs. Martin from her father. She'd been a customer at the garage and she'd been coming to buy a bouquet for as long as Andi had worked at In Bloom. She was sweet and endearing, and Andi had a hunch she knew more about her life, thanks to her dad's propensity for gossip, than she was comfortable with others knowing. But her father and Mrs. Martin's husband had been good friends and the older woman had a good heart.

"Hi, Mrs. Martin," Andi said.

"How are you today?" the other woman asked.

Andi smiled. "I'm fine. And you?"

She patted her gray hair. "I just came from the salon. It always puts me in a good mood. Now who was that nice gentleman you were talking to? He looked familiar."

Andi swallowed hard, hoping the older woman hadn't caught her ogling Kyle as he left. "Kyle Davenport. Maybe you know his parents? Henry and Darla? His father used to own the hardware store."

"Oh, yes. Of course. He looks just like his father. Nice-looking men, both of them. Don't you think?"

Andi blushed and nodded. "Yes, he is." And each time she saw him, she was struck anew by how attractive she found him.

Today, in his usual button-down shirt, this one cream, and dark slacks, she found him both preppy and sexy at the same time.

The older woman sighed. "I miss my Sam," she said of her late husband. "If I could give advice to you young people, it would be to enjoy and appreciate every day with the person you love because you don't know how long you'll have."

"That's a beautiful and true statement," Andi murmured. She'd just never found the man she loved.

By the time she realized what a mistake she'd made with Billy, he'd had a tight hold on her. She'd gotten pregnant right after graduation and missed out on going to college, tying herself to her baby's father when in reality she'd already been scared of him and should have had the courage to walk away.

She sighed. "Not everyone finds the right man though," she found herself saying.

Wise, old blue eyes looked back at her. "Sometimes you have to open your eyes and see what's in front of you without fear blocking your way."

Yes, Mrs. Martin knew too much, Andi thought. "So what can I get for you today? The usual?" she asked, although the woman never varied her choice.

"Yes. The same bouquet for Sam."

Andi already had the arrangement made and put aside for her regular customer. She collected payment, cash as usual, and handed Mrs. Martin her purchase. "Here you go."

"Thank you, dear. Say hello to your father for me. It's been a while since I've seen him."

"I will. Enjoy your visit with your husband," she said, because Mrs. Martin always told her that these visits and talks she had were cathartic.

She watched the older woman go, her heart heavy with the knowledge that she'd given up any chance to real relationship happiness in her life. She no longer trusted her judgment when it came to the opposite sex.

THE REST OF the week passed quickly and Friday arrived and with it the much-needed weekend. Kyle loved his students but he appreciated the Saturday-Sunday break as much as anyone.

Knowing the move was a permanent one, Kyle had bought a house when he moved back to Rosewood Bay. But that didn't mean his mother didn't expect him to show up for occasional meals, and given his poor cooking skills, he considered Sunday dinner one of the perks of coming home.

This week, they were getting together on Saturday instead to celebrate his mom's birthday. Kyle and his brother, Chase, had wanted to take her out for dinner but she insisted on having the whole family at home. He arrived midafternoon and spent time with his dad before gravitating into the kitchen, where his mother put him to work chopping lettuce for the salad while Chase set the table. Although she was past her broken hip, her gait was slower now, as she was more careful in how she moved.

When Kyle had entered the room, she had been grilling Chase about his social life and any women he might be dating.

"Mom, have you been keeping up with your exercises?" Chase asked, making a deliberate subject change.

His mother nodded. "Not only have I, but I've signed up for swim classes at the local Y. The doctor said that will be good for overall conditioning."

"Sounds good. Can you get Dad to go with you? He could use some exercise," Kyle said.

His mother laughed at that. "You know better. Now stop changing the subject, boys. Kyle, how do you like your class?" she asked as she wiped her hands on a dish towel.

"The kids are great. Everything's going well."

"Do you have any of your old friends' children?" she asked.

His gaze darted to hers. Did she know he had Andi's son in his class? He doubted she knew the boy's exact age and grade, but he wouldn't put it past her to be curious enough to ferret out the information this way. He didn't particularly want to get into a discussion about Andi Harmon, but if he didn't mention Nicky and his mother found out, she'd never let him hear the end of it.

He dumped the cut lettuce into the bowl and met his mother's gaze. "Andi Harmon's son is in my class," he told her, not reacting in any way. Instead he picked up a washed tomato and began to slice.

"Well, that should be interesting."

Chase snickered from where he'd settled into a chair at the table.

Kyle shot him a dirty look.

"When will you have to see her? Parent-teacher night?" His mom leaned against the counter, wholly interested in the conversation.

"Darla, leave the boys alone," his father called from the other room, where he sat in his recliner watching television.

"It's just a question," his mom called back.

Kyle sighed. "I've seen her a few times already. We had to discuss certain things about her son. It was fine, Mom. We're adults."

"You never told me exactly what happened between the two of you to end a lifelong friendship, but I always felt sorry for her."

"She married an asshole," Chase chimed in not so helpfully. He spoke the truth though. "It's hard to imagine her not knowing what she was getting into."

"Well, she always struck me as a lonely woman," his mother said. "Kyle wasn't the only friend she lost over the years. I think she paid for her choices. And not in any good way."

He glanced up from his focus on the knife in his hands. He had that sense himself. Still, he couldn't help but feel, like Chase, that she'd knowingly made her own decisions. "She had enough experience with Billy to know who he was."

"Boys, I raised you to be more compassionate. From what I saw, Billy had complete control over her. From who she saw to where she went. And I think she dressed to cover bruises."

Kyle's stomach turned over. He was unable to believe she'd been abused and he'd had no idea. "What?"

His mom nodded somberly. "You never wanted to talk about Andi, so I didn't say anything. She obviously didn't want anyone to know, and though I always told her she could talk to me about anything, she never took me up on it."

At the thought of Billy putting a hand on Andi, fury raced through Kyle, along with anger at himself for not realizing the extent of what she'd gotten herself into with her ex. He'd been so busy being hurt and upset with her for dumping him, he'd never given a thought to the whys. Of course, they'd been young, and he hadn't had enough life experience to even think that Billy would hurt her. Though Billy had been a bully, it had never dawned on Kyle that the relationship was abusive.

"Shit." He dumped the tomato in with the rest of the salad, his mood ruined. He couldn't very well hold on to anger at her breaking off a friendship when she'd been dealing with something far beyond anything he could have imagined.

He finished making the salad in silence, his mother obviously having sensed she'd crossed a sensitive line and he needed time to process what she'd told him. Meanwhile, his head pounded, the information eating away at his gut.

The doorbell rang, providing a welcome break. "I'll get it," he said, eager to escape his thoughts.

Hopefully it was the flowers he'd asked to be delivered for his mom, since they hadn't arrived yet. He opened the door to find Andi standing with the beautiful bouquet in her hands.

"Kyle!" she said, obviously as surprised to see him as he was to see her. "Delivery, as promised."

He took the vase full of fall-colored flowers from her hand, orange, yellow, and deep red hues blossoming inside. "These are beautiful. Thank you. I thought you had a delivery guy to handle this?"

She sighed. "So did I but he bailed. I have a seventeen-year-old covering the store. Deliveries aren't her job, so I'm doing them myself today."

She really did work hard, he thought, wondering how she also found time to be with her son. His heart gave a little squeeze at the thought of her running herself ragged while her abusive ex was off God knows where. Town rumor said he'd run off with one of the wealthy women who frequented their beach town in the summers, leaving his family behind.

"Well, thank you for making sure my mom got these as promised." Should he tip her? It felt awkward and he had a feeling he shouldn't, but she worked so damned hard for whatever she had. He reached into his pocket and pulled out his money clip, but before he could peel off bills, Andi glanced down and saw his intention.

"Kyle, please. Don't," she said, her cheeks red with embarrassment.

"Kyle, who is it?" His mother came out of the kitchen, ending the uncomfortable exchange. Her eyes widened, then lit up at the sight of the flowers. And then she laid eyes on Andi and her happy smile broadened. "Andrea! It's so good to see you."

"Hi, Mrs. Davenport. Happy birthday!"

"It's Darla, not Mrs. Davenport. I tell you that every time we run into each other." She rushed over to give Andi a hug.

"I was just delivering your flowers. I hope you enjoy them," Andi said, and turned to go.

"Wait. Come in and chat for a little while."

Andi shook her head. "I can't. Thank you but–"

"Nonsense." Persistent as ever, his mom grasped her hand and urged her to come into the house.

"Mom, Andi has to work."

"She has a few minutes to talk to old friends." Holding on to Andi, she led her into the kitchen.

Andi's eyes met his. "I'm sorry," she mouthed, obviously believing he didn't want her there.

To his surprise, he didn't mind her staying, although his mother should have respected her wishes and let her leave. But then she wouldn't be his loving albeit intrusive mom.

He followed Andi and his mother into the kitchen, his gaze on Andi's tight jeans and the sexy sway of her hips as she moved. She was unaware of her appeal, much as she had been as a teen, although she'd been more outgoing and happier back then. She was more reserved now, her marriage obviously having changed her and, as his mother had pointed out, not in good ways.

"Can I get you a drink? I have soda in the fridge," his mom offered.

"It's fine. I really can't stay long," Andi said, but his mother headed to the refrigerator and poured her a drink anyway.

"Mom, I'm putting the flowers by the sink," Kyle said.

He noted Chase had disappeared, probably watching television with his father and saying a prayer of thanks it was Kyle's life his mother was meddling in and not his own.

"They're just so beautiful. Did you put them together yourself?" his mom asked.

Andi nodded, taking a sip of her soda, then running her tongue over her damp lips. He forced his gaze onto something else. *Flowers. Look at the flowers.*

"Wendy, the owner, taught me how to arrange them," Andi said, pointing to the blooms.

"Well, you have a talent for it, that's for sure, doesn't she, Kyle?"

"She sure does," he said, meaning it.

His mother walked over to the arrangement and breathed in deep. "They smell glorious."

"I'm glad you like them," Andi said, placing her glass down on the counter. "Well, I should get–"

"Let me go get Henry and show him how gorgeous they are," his mother said, ignoring Andi's attempt to leave. She turned and headed out to the family room, leaving them alone.

He met her gaze, unable to help the grin on his face. "She's as subtle as a steamroller," he said. "I am sorry. I can sneak you out before she returns."

Andi laughed, the sound bringing back old memories of the times they'd been relaxed and comfortable around each other. He could admit to himself now that he missed those days, and he pushed hard at the sting of rejection that wanted to resurface, knowing now there had been more to what she had been going through.

"I should really say goodbye to her. It's the polite thing to do," Andi said.

"Trust me, she'll never let you escape. Come on." Aware she needed to get back to the store, he led her to the door. "Listen, when you come to pick up Nicky next time, can the three of us go over some things?"

"Of course. I'll be there to pick him up on Tuesday." She smiled. "It was good seeing you and your mom."

"Thanks for the flowers. They really are beautiful." Just like she was, he thought, unable not to be drawn to her.

She smiled. "Thanks again. And tell your mother I appreciate the hospitality but I needed to get back to work. I hate to have her thinking I'm rude."

"I will and I'll see you on Tuesday."

"Great." She ducked her head and strode out.

He watched her go, a pit of longing in his stomach, warning bells ringing in his brain. This woman had owned him once before and ripped his heart out of his chest. He couldn't afford to let her do it again, but every time he saw her, he softened toward her even more.

AFTER A BUSY day at the floral shop, including helping a couple planning their engagement party and putting together a funeral arrangement and a few birthday bouquets, Andi was exhausted. She still had to pick Nicky up after school, meet with Kyle, and figure out something for dinner.

She walked into the school, checked in at the security desk, and headed to Kyle's classroom. At a glance, she saw him sitting beside Nicky, wholly focused on her son and his reading. He leaned one muscular forearm on the back of a chair, the other hand pointing to the paper from which Nicky read. She watched, her heart engaged at the sight. Although she understood he was just doing his job, this was her baby he was helping, and gratitude and desire continued to fight each time she ran into him.

She cleared her throat so they'd know she was there.

Nicky glanced up, smiling when he saw her. "Hey, Mom."

"Hi," Kyle said, his sexy mouth widening into a smile as he looked up, his eyes warming as they roamed over her.

"Hi." She walked into the room and stopped by the desks where they worked. "How's it going?"

"Great! We worked on my reading." Nicky gathered his papers from his desk.

"I'm really happy with how far he's progressed," Kyle said.

Nicky walked over to the far wall and began to put together his jacket and books.

"You wanted to talk?" she asked.

"I introduced him to *Harry Potter*. I'm hoping it will engage him in reading and I can work with the comprehension when he stays after school with me."

She nodded. "Absolutely. Whatever you suggest." There was no bookstore in town, so she'd order a copy online.

"Mom, I'm starving," Nicky said, skidding to a stop in front of her, backpack slung over his shoulder.

"What do you say we stop for a really early pizza dinner before we go home?" She didn't have the energy to make anything tonight and she hadn't put anything in the crockpot this morning.

"Score!" he said, obviously thrilled with the idea.

She glanced at Kyle, who'd walked over to his desk and had begun to pack things up in a duffel bag. "Would you like to join us?" she found herself asking. "I know it's not even five o'clock yet, but there are nights I just say go with the flow and tonight is one of them. My treat." She gave him a welcoming smile.

It was the least she could do for the effort he was making with Nicky. She told herself she'd do the same for any of his teachers, but the rapid pounding of her heart threatened to make that statement a lie. She wanted time with him to catch up and maybe become friends again.

He hesitated, obviously unsure what to say. He'd been warmer at his mother's house, his reaction to her more relaxed and easier with each run-in, and she hoped to build on that foundation.

"Come on, Mr. D. That would be cool," Nicky said, seconding her invitation.

He glanced from her to her son. "Sure, why not? I'll meet you at the pizza place in town," he said of Rosa's Pizzeria.

"Sounds good."

She and Nicky headed to the car. The entire ride into town, he talked about how excited he was to go out with Mr. D, the kids' nickname for their teacher. Kyle had a way about him that didn't make Nicky feel singled out or different because he needed extra help. Nicky missed out on having a father but since Billy had been gone, her brother had been a solid role model in his life and now he had Kyle as a man he could look up to and learn from. She warmed at the thought.

They waited for Kyle at a table, the place fairly empty thanks to the early hour. He joined them, sliding into the booth. "I love Hawaiian pizza," Nicky said to him. "Do you?"

"What's in it?" Kyle asked.

Andi bit down on the inside of her cheek. Hawaiian pizza was an acquired taste. "Pineapple and bacon. Or ham but Nicky likes his with bacon," she explained. "I think it's the combination of sweet, sour, and salty that he finds appealing."

Kyle made a disgusted face. "I think I'll pass."

"You have to at least taste it," Nicky said. "Can I go order, Mom?"

"Do you still like mushroom and onion on yours?" Andi asked Kyle.

He blinked, as if startled she remembered. "Yeah."

"Order a large, half Hawaiian, half mushroom and onion," she told him. "And a pitcher of Diet Coke?" she asked Kyle and he nodded.

"Someone has to have a talk with the Hawaiians about that pizza topping," he muttered.

"Actually it originated in Canada."

He raised an eyebrow.

"I saw it on *Jeopardy*," she said with a grin.

"All set." Nicky bounced back to their table and slid in beside her.

"Mom, how'd you know what Mr. D. likes on his pizza?" Nicky, her smart boy, asked, obviously having picked up on her question.

"We … grew up together," she said.

"Your mom and I used to be really good friends," Kyle said. "Before I moved away for college." His golden-brown gaze locked with hers, the basic truth passing between them.

Before she'd pushed him away. But he protected her son from the way she'd broken something so precious between them, and she appreciated his sensitivity.

"Cool!" Nicky said. "You didn't tell me you guys knew each other."

"It never came up," she murmured. "So I hear you're going to be reading *Harry Potter*. What if I reread it? We can talk about it at home, too," she said.

"Yeah. I like that," Nicky said.

Kyle shot her a warm look accompanied by an appreciative nod. Obviously he thought she was handling Nicky's reading issues the right way and she was glad.

"What was my mom like when she was younger?" Nicky asked out of the blue, surprising her.

Kyle blinked. "Well, let's see. She was fun and happy, and she laughed. A lot."

Nicky wrinkled his nose. "That doesn't sound like my mom. You're always so serious," her son said to her, the words hitting her like a punch in the stomach.

Was that how her little boy saw her? Serious, not laughing or enjoying life? That wasn't the impression she wanted to give him. But the truth was she had lost the lightness of being a while ago and she had Billy – and herself – to blame.

"It's serious business being a parent," Kyle said, jumping in in the wake of her silence. "Your mom has a lot on her shoulders."

She appreciated his explanation, but she made a silent promise to smile and laugh more around her son. "Being an adult is very different than being a kid," she agreed. "But I vote we have more fun together from now on."

Nicky grinned. "I like that idea."

A waitress brought the pizza to the table, which thankfully changed the subject. They talked football, the New England Patriots being the team of choice, and Nicky encouraged Kyle to try his Hawaiian pizza, which he did with good humor. But he didn't love the combined taste.

"Kyle? Davenport!" A man Andi recognized as Ryan Mueller, one of Kyle's old high school friends and someone Andi had been friendly with as well, walked over to the table. "I heard you were back in town."

"Hey, Ryan." Kyle pushed out of the booth and shook the other man's hand. "It's been a long time.

What have you been doing with yourself?"

"I'm an attorney. You?"

"Teacher," Kyle said. "Nicky here is one of my students. And you must remember Andi Harmon."

Ryan ran a hand through his blond hair and nodded. "Andi! Where have you been hiding?"

"I've been busy working at In Bloom and of course with this guy." She gestured to Nicky, who was drinking his soda, not paying attention to the adult conversation around him.

"Hey, I'm having some people over to watch the football game on Sunday," Ryan said. "Why don't you two join us? I'm seeing Nina Jones now and you two used to be close. I'm sure she'd love to see you," he said to Andi.

She bit down on the inside of her cheek. "Oh, I don't know. I have Nicky and–"

"I'm going to Uncle Kane's to watch the game, remember, Mom?" Obviously she'd been wrong and he had been paying attention.

"Right." So much for that excuse. "I appreciate the invitation–"

"Great. We'll look forward to seeing you." Ryan jumped to the conclusion that she'd be there. "Kyle? What about you?"

"Love to," he said with a smile. "It'll be good to catch up."

"Twenty-five Old Mill Road. Around four p.m. See you both then." Ryan turned and headed back to the counter where he'd been ordering food.

"Guess we're going to a football party." Kyle rolled his shoulders, the muscles moving in an enticing stretch and flex. "I haven't seen many people since I've been back. I'm looking forward to reconnecting."

She, on the other hand, wasn't so comfortable with small talk and connections. Not since high school had she had close girlfriends. When she was married to Billy, she'd always felt like people were looking at her, wondering about her long sleeves to cover bruises, and were aware that she'd isolated herself and were curious about why. Although it had been two years since he'd disappeared from her life, she still preferred to keep to herself and not answer questions about things she didn't want to talk about or admit to.

But she was going to a football party and she'd try to get herself back out into the world of adults again with only Kyle as her anchor.

Chapter Three

ANDI TRIED TO think of every excuse in the world not to go to the party. She hadn't seen Nina and her friends, once Andi's friends, since her pre-Billy days, another casualty thanks to her poor choices. But in the end, she knew she needed to put on her big-girl panties and show up. What kind of example would she be setting for her son if she backed out? The worst thing that could happen was someone asking her about Billy, and she could handle that. She hoped.

She put on a pair of jeans and a New England Patriots football jersey and a pair of sneakers. A quick glance in the mirror told her that her hair was presentable, makeup minimal, and she was ready to go. "Come on, Nicky! I'll drop you off at Uncle Kane and Aunt Halley's on the way to my party."

He joined her, dressed in a jersey of his own, his hair spiky and standing on end, the way he liked it. She held back a grin, knowing she couldn't tell him she thought he was cute.

"I'm ready. Can I stay with Uncle Kane for dinner?" he asked.

She nodded, grateful her son had Kane as a male influence in his life. His father certainly hadn't been a positive role model when he'd been around, belittling him but thankfully saving the real hands-on abuse for Andi. She'd like to think if he'd touched her child, she would have been out of there.

Shaking her head at her train of thought, she refocused on Nicky's question. The game was at four o'clock and would run past dinner. "Yes. I'll pick you up when the game is over."

"Is Grandpa going to be there?"

"I'm not sure." Her dad was back to gambling, which meant she didn't know where he'd be and when, especially on the weekends, just one of the reasons she'd taken Nicky and moved into a place of her own after years of living in her dad's house. The same house she'd grown up in.

Her stomach churned at the thought of his addiction, but she'd long since accepted she couldn't change him. "All your homework is finished, right?" she asked Nicky, switching the subject.

"Yeah, including the first chapters of *Harry Potter.*"

"Then we can go." She dropped him off at her brother's house on the beach, walking him in and spending some time with Kane and Halley before heading out to Ryan's house. Cars lined the street, telling her she wasn't the first one there, and she saw

Kyle's Ford Explorer parked by the mailbox, and some of the nerves in her stomach relaxed, knowing there was a familiar, friendly face waiting inside.

Thanks to their pizza dinner, she felt as if the ice between them had thawed, and even if he was angry at her for the past, they'd managed to put it behind them enough to be nice to each other. And she needed that support right now.

She drew a deep breath, walked up to the front door, and rang the bell. A familiar pretty brunette with dark brown hair and eyes answered the door. "Andi! Ryan told me you'd be coming by and I was so happy he ran into you!"

"Hi, Nina. It's good to see you. You look wonderful."

The other woman smiled. "Thanks. So do you. Come on in! Some of the girls are here." She led Andi into the kitchen, bypassing the family room, where the men were congregated for the game.

"Hey, everyone, look who's here," Nina called out to the women.

A bunch of eyes turned Andi's way. "Hi," she said with an awkward wave.

"You know everyone," Nina said. "It's just been a while."

Andi nodded. Although she hadn't kept up with them personally, in her small town, she couldn't help but hear about people through the grapevine or run into them on occasion. She knew some of the women were married, others were still single, and one, like Andi, was divorced.

"Andi, how have you been?" Cynthia Colson, a pretty redhead, asked.

"Busy, what with my son starting fourth grade, and working during the day. But it's all good. How about you?"

"I recently got engaged!" She wriggled her hand with a nice-sized ring for everyone to see. "Daniel Scott is my fiancé."

"Congratulations!" Andi said. She remembered Daniel from high school, a quiet guy with a good sense of humor. "What does he do now?"

"He's a financial officer at the bank and I'm a teller there, which you know from coming in. We reconnected one night at a holiday party... and that was that."

"I'm happy for you," Andi said.

"I heard you got divorced," Cynthia said, her gaze still on her ring.

Andi bit the inside of her cheek, not surprised the subject came up. "We've been apart for almost two years."

"That's hard," the newly engaged woman said. "Nobody goes into a marriage expecting it to end. I can't even imagine." She spoke as if she were trying to ward off Andi's bad luck in her own life. "Then again, if my husband was sleeping around with Maya Dane while I was pregnant, I would have been well rid of him, too."

Andi blinked, Cynthia's words hitting her with the force of a freight train. "I'm sorry, what did you say?" She could add cheating to Billy's list of sins? While she was pregnant with his son?

She broke out into a cold sweat, feeling like the stupid, oblivious wife. When he'd started to leave her alone sexually, she'd been relieved. Her pregnancy hadn't been an easy one and by that time, Billy's temper made him someone she didn't want around her on a good day. She'd known he'd go out to drink but she'd never thought he was cheating.

Nina caught Andi's gaze, her eyes wide and horrified. "Hey, let's go into the family room. The game started." She grabbed Andi's hand and started to pull her away from the oblivious and clearly tactless Cynthia.

"Andi, wait," Janie Hudson, a woman Andi had been very close with in high school, said.

"You sure you're okay?" Nina asked.

Andi nodded. "I'm fine. No need to worry about me, but thank you." She turned to Janie. "Hi," she said to her old friend.

Janie smiled. "I'm really glad you came today. It's been too long."

Andi nodded. She agreed. There'd been times she missed Janie and thought about calling, renewing the friendship. But what would she have said by way of explanation? *Billy didn't like me to have friends but I'm rid of him and back now?* Talk about mortifying. So she'd never reached out.

"It's good to see you, too. How's the job?" Andi asked.

Janie worked as a vet tech for Dr. Canon, the town's veterinarian.

"I still love animals, so it's great. How's the floral shop?" Janie asked, taking a sip of the drink in her hand.

"Good. I really found my niche there," Andi said, knowing she was lucky her job was something she loved.

"Listen… about what Cynthia said…"

Andi stiffened. It was bad enough she'd found out Billy had been cheating, but to have to discuss it with a woman she hadn't seen in years? It was too much.

But in her heart, she knew Janie meant well. "My marriage wasn't a good one and more people were aware of it than I ever realized," she murmured. "Though I haven't been out mingling in a while, I hoped it wouldn't be the central topic of conversation."

Janie smiled in understanding. "It isn't. That's what I wanted to tell you. Everyone has their own garbage in life to deal with and knows better than to bring up difficult subjects. Cynthia is just very self-centered, like Nina said."

"Thank you," Andi said. She appreciated Janie's sensitivity.

"I'm just happy to see you and I hope we can get together, maybe for lunch or something?" the other woman asked hopefully.

Andi smiled. "Sure. I'd like that."

"Want to check out the game?" Janie asked and Andi nodded.

"I'm happy to watch Tom Brady," she said, laughing.

She and Janie walked into the other room, a large area with a flat-screen television on the wall and a comfortable-looking reclining sofa in the center.

The men were spread around, some on the couch, others in small groups talking amongst themselves. And by the bay window, Kyle was holding a drink and chatting up a very pretty, clearly interested-in-him woman Andi remembered from high school named Kimberly Greene.

She'd been a sex-driven siren back in the day, and from the way she shook out her long blonde hair when she laughed, combined with her tight jeans and cropped top now, not much had changed. Except for the fact that Kyle appeared extremely interested in what she was saying.

Watching them interact, Kimberly's hand on his chest as she laughed at something he said, Andi's stomach twisted uncomfortably. Until now, she'd thought her awareness of Kyle was a superficial thing, something she could brush aside as unimportant. But her jealous reaction to seeing him with another woman told her very clearly she'd been wrong.

The feelings she had for him weren't all about old friendship and included an attraction she hadn't counted on experiencing. She might not desire a relationship at this point in her life, but she certainly desired Kyle, a man who was tolerating her at best, being civil to her because of her son.

Between the revelation about her cheating ex and now watching Kyle eagerly engaged with another woman, she'd had just about all she could take of her first public outing in years. But she refused to admit defeat, so a quick trip to the ladies' room to freshen up and pull herself together was in order.

She took one more look at Kyle, appearing very serious about something Kimberly said to him. He reached out and put a hand on her shoulder and she leaned in closer. Andi's stomach churned and she spun around, making her way to the bathroom, hoping she could calm herself down and make herself presentable again.

KYLE COULDN'T TEAR himself away from Kimberly Greene, who had pulled him aside from the moment he'd walked into the house. He'd wanted to hang out with guys he hadn't seen in a while, grab a beer, and watch the game. But Kimberly had intercepted him and held him hostage. To make matters worse, her brother had cancer, and when she realized she was losing him on a sexual interest level, because he'd been perfectly clear he wasn't interested, she'd turned on the emotional waterworks to keep him by her side.

He sympathized with her pain over her brother's situation, but it wasn't going to change the lack of attraction on his end.

When Andi walked into the room, looking surprisingly sexy in her Brady jersey, her luscious hair tumbling over her shoulders and her vulnerability stark for him to see, he couldn't tear his gaze away. She obviously wasn't comfortable here and he felt bad for her. He knew Ryan had cornered her into coming today, and though he meant well, Andi obviously hadn't socialized with these people in a long time. The crowded house must be overwhelming to her.

He turned in time to see her glance at him, pivot, and head toward the back of the house, where the bathroom was located. Worried because she'd looked upset, he excused himself from Kimberly and followed Andi, winding his way past people who hadn't yet settled in to watch the game.

He caught up in time to see the bathroom door close and he waited outside for her to come back out. It didn't take long for her to reopen the door. He immediately noticed her eyes were red from crying.

"Kyle, hi." She forced a smile and stepped aside as if to let him pass and go in.

"Before you walk away, let's talk." He grasped her wrist and pulled her into the small bathroom.

"What are you doing?" she asked as he closed the door behind them.

"You're upset and I want to know why."

She bit down on her trembling lower lip. "It's nothing."

He brushed his hand over her damp cheek. "It's not nothing. Did someone say something to set you off?"

She lifted one shoulder. "Cynthia Colson mentioned something about Billy sleeping with Maya Dane while I was pregnant with Nicky." She drew in a shuddering breath. "You know what they say. The wife is always the last to know."

He winced at the relayed information. "Stupid bastard," he said of her ex-husband.

"I'm not even upset because he cheated on me, per se. I'm angry with myself for being so blind. The truth is, I was so relieved he wasn't touching me back then, I never stopped to ask myself why," she said without meeting his gaze.

He placed a hand beneath her chin and lifted her face so she had no choice but to look at him and face the things she was admitting to. "Your marriage sucked."

"More than you know."

I told you so was the last thing she needed to hear, so he didn't say it. "It was stupid of Cynthia to bring it up," he muttered.

"She seems to be oblivious to anything but her own happiness." She shrugged. "It's fine. I just got hit by an overwhelming amount of emotions at one time. I'm okay now. Thanks for checking on me. I didn't mean to drag you away from Kimberly. You two seemed to be hitting it off."

He didn't pull his hand away from her face, struck by the tinge of something in her voice. Jealousy? And if so, why did it please him that she cared?

"Kimberly was like a leech who wouldn't let go. She even used her sick brother's story to hang on to me. I wasn't doing anything more than offering sympathy," he said, opting for the truth.

Andi blinked, unmistakable relief in her pretty brown eyes. "Really?"

"Did it bother you when you thought I was into her?" he heard himself asking, knowing he hadn't planned to go down this road, but the attraction between them was a real, tangible thing.

His fingers itched to run through her thick, wavy hair, and he couldn't tear his gaze from her glossed lips as she ran her tongue nervously over them. Not to mention the energy it took not to look down at her full breasts beneath the jersey.

"Would it upset you if I said it did? That watching you with her stirred up feelings that took me by surprise?"

"I shouldn't want you, Andi. You hurt me. Took a fucking knife to my heart. But that was in the past. And what's going on now between us is the present."

Her eyes shimmered with unshed tears, the past alive despite them both wanting to put it behind them. But everything inside him was pulled toward her now, drawn to her fragile strength and beauty.

He dipped his head and pressed his mouth to hers. Warm and giving, her soft lips moved beneath his. His hand slid around her jaw, tilting her head, giving him better access as his tongue delved into her mouth and tangled with hers. Finally, finally, finally, finally. His heart beat out the word in rapid rhythm, a long-held desire coming true as her kiss turned him inside out.

He explored the deep recesses of her mouth, tasting her essence, aware of his body's reaction, the swell of his cock behind his jeans, the spike in adrenaline, the racing of his pulse.

Despite the pain, the anger, the hurt, this was the girl of his dreams and she was in his arms, eagerly accepting his kiss. He slid his hand into her hair, grasping the thick strands between his fingers and tugging as the kiss turned hotter and he backed her against the vanity, his waist flush against hers, his hard erection cradled between her thighs. His cock throbbed with unappeased need, desire flowing between them.

Until a hard knock sounded on the door, startling them into breaking apart. She looked at him, wide-eyed, the surprise etched in her face as strong as the shock rippling through him.

"Be right out," he called to the person on the other side of the door.

He glanced at Andi, her face now flushed a bright red. "There's no way to avoid walking out together, is there?" she asked.

"Whether you go first or last, whoever it is heard my voice."

Her blush deepened. "Well, then here's to giving

them something more to talk about," she said, straightening her shoulders.

Admiring her grit, he not-so-discreetly adjusted his junk in his pants. "No time like the present," he said and reached for the door handle.

With his hand on her back so as not to leave her dealing with embarrassment alone, he led her out of the restroom to find Kimberly waiting outside in the hall.

"Kyle!" she said, her gaze darting over his shoulder to Andi. "Oh." Her smile disappeared as she took in the obvious situation.

Knowing there were no words that were going to make this less awkward, he pulled Andi with him down the hall as Kimberly slammed the bathroom door behind her.

He didn't spend time with Andi the rest of the night, she mingling with the women, he hanging with the guys and watching the game. But he couldn't deny he was aware of her the entire time, knew where in the room she stood, with whom she was speaking. The kiss between them had changed their dynamic. No longer did he consider her someone for whom he held on to long-suppressed anger. She was a woman he desired. And he had to figure out what to do with that.

✧　✧　✧

THE NEXT WEEK passed in a blur, Kyle's kiss never far from Andi's mind. She woke up early each day, showered and dressed, made her son breakfast, and helped him get ready for school. She dropped him off and spent the day at In Bloom. Whether she was cutting or arranging flowers, making a sale, or planning the décor for a party, the feel of his lips on hers was a constant distraction.

Their chemistry was such a new thing, something she'd never thought about before when it came to Kyle, but now she felt as if it was consuming her. The idea of wanting Kyle threw her because it had been so long since she'd desired any man. She'd thought she'd shut off those feelings, well aware that insulating herself and keeping her distance was safer both physically and emotionally.

Yet she couldn't stop thinking of him. Of the way he'd grown into himself, his shoulders broad, his muscles well defined, telling her he obviously went to the gym in his free time. He was handsome, with his strong jaw and sculpted cheekbones, and one adorable dimple in his cheek.

He was putting the past behind them, albeit slowly, and for that she was grateful. But the yearning she felt for him wasn't welcome. She didn't have room for any man in her life, not when she had a son to raise and a past to outrun. She didn't want another man potentially telling her what to do, who she could see, what she could do. She had spent the last two years rebuilding her independence and she intended to keep it.

No matter how tempting Kyle Davenport happened to be.

As the week wound to a close, her monthly dreaded dinner with her ex-mother-in-law was coming up quickly. She took Nicky to see Billy's mom once a month, and though she knew he was at an age where he could go alone, it made her feel better to be there and monitor what her ex-mother-in-law said about Nicky's father. The truth was, Francine Gray was a lovely woman who, despite having raised her child right, had ended up with an egotistical, abusive bastard for a son. Billy's father had died a few years ago, and he, too, had been a decent man. Andi had no problem allowing her son to know his grandparents, but under no circumstances did she want Francine talking up her son as a good man.

He'd never wanted a child, had resented Andi for getting pregnant and refusing to get rid of her baby. After he was born, he'd wanted nothing to do with his son. To Billy, Nicky just tied him down further. And though it hurt Andi for Nicky to know the truth about his father, he had lived in this house and seen it all. She hadn't been able to protect him from Billy's anger then, the emotional abuse as bad for her child as the physical he'd heaped on Andi, and she didn't want his grandmother's words swaying him toward wanting to see his father again. Just because Billy hadn't turned on Nicky physically in the past didn't mean he wouldn't in the future should he return.

She shivered at the possibility and immediately put it out of her mind. He'd given her full custody and that allowed her to protect him.

They arrived at Francine's house, a run-down ranch that had seen better days. A lot of work needed to be done on the house to make it more livable, but there was no one to do it. Even when Billy had been in town, he hadn't prioritized his mother's living situation and the house was in desperate need of repair.

Francine met them at the door, a wide smile on her face, her blonde hair cut shorter than usual. "Andi, Nicky!" She opened her arms and pulled her grandson into a hug.

"Hi, Grandma." Nicky hugged her back. "Did you make my favorite lasagna?" he asked.

She kissed the top of his head. "You know I did. Come on in."

They followed her into the family room, Andi bracing herself for the photos of her ex-husband around the room, at various stages of his life. Just looking at him brought back unpleasant, painful memories and she put blinders on as she settled onto the floral couch.

"Nicky, tell me about school," Francine said.

"I have the best teacher. Mr. D. is helping me with my reading. I'm reading *Harry Potter* and I love it," he said, and went off about the story.

When he finished talking about the book, he continued on about *Mr. D. said this*, and *Mr. D. said that*. Even if Andi had wanted to put Kyle out of her mind, Nicky made it impossible.

"This Mr. D. sounds really special," Francine said.

"He's amazing. All my friends think so." Which explained why the extra help wasn't causing Nicky to be made fun of by the other kids.

"I often wonder if my William had had a teacher to look up to, if he would have turned out to be a better man. Samuel wasn't all that involved with him," she said of Billy's father. "And that football coach was so hard on him all the time, expecting perfection..." Francine caught Andi's wide-eyed gaze and shake of her head and trailed off. "Sorry."

Andi glanced at Nicky.

"Dad used to yell at me. A lot," he said, his shoulders slumping as they usually did at any mention of his father.

Andi closed her eyes and sighed. If there was anything in her life she didn't want to revisit, it was how Billy had treated his son. She'd take all the wrist twists and hard shoves and hits if it meant she was protecting Nicky. But verbally, Billy hadn't discriminated. He'd always been angry and always taken it out on them both.

"Well, he's not around to do that anymore," Andi said, not worrying about her one-time mother-in-law's feelings. She couldn't do that and put Nicky first.

"Let's eat," Francine said, changing the subject, for which Andi was grateful.

The rest of the meal passed peacefully without another mention of Billy, but Nicky had quieted down a lot. Not even his enthusiasm over Mr. D. remained, and when they arrived home, he wasn't in the mood to read an extra chapter of his book.

She waited until he'd showered for school the next day and walked into his room. He was curled in his bed beneath his navy comforter, playing on an iPad.

"Hey, Nicky. Everything okay?"

He shrugged.

She sat down on the edge of the bed. "Did something Grandma Francine say upset you?" she asked, diving into the deep end of what she thought was bothering him.

"Grandma sounds like she makes excuses for Dad. Like if his coach hadn't been mean, then he wouldn't have been either. But…"

Andi waited for him to gather his thoughts and

continue. When he didn't, she asked, "But what?"

He bit down on his bottom lip. "But I had a mean teacher last year and I was still nice to my friends."

She smiled at her wise-beyond-his-years son, wishing he was able to just be a kid. "You're right. How someone else treats you is no excuse for how you behave. You should always take the high road."

"Mom?"

"Yes?" She bent a knee beneath her and looked him in the eye.

"Dad's never coming back, right?" He dropped his gaze from hers, clearly mortified by the question.

"Hey. Look at me." She scooted closer to him, sitting cross-legged on the bed. Under any other circumstances, she'd spare him legalities, but she didn't want him to worry about Billy's possible return. "Even if he comes back, I have what's called legal full custody. He would need my permission to see you and that's not happening."

Billy could take her to court. He could threaten and bully her. She'd be doing what was best for her son and he was thriving in the absence of his father, his shoulders no longer slumping, no longer skulking around corners, worried his dad was there to yell at him. She had enough people to testify to the fact that his father not being in his life was in Nicky's best interest.

He threw his arms around her neck and hugged her tight. "I feel bad that I don't want him to come back."

"He caused that, not you." She wrapped her arms around him tight. "Don't worry, okay? That's my job for both of us."

She'd go to the ends of the earth to protect him and see the smile he had on his face when he talked about the teacher he loved.

Chapter Four

EVER SINCE THE football party, Kyle's thoughts about Andi had shifted and not just because he'd kissed her, although he had to admit he'd replayed the moment over in his mind. He was jumbled up inside, trying to reconcile his anger at her over the past and his feelings for her now.

For years he'd wondered how she'd feel in his arms. Her soft lips and lithe body were the answer to his dreams, and everything he saw in her personality made it difficult for him to be angry with her in any way. In fact, something didn't add up. The woman who'd told him to go away and leave her alone was nowhere to be found. The Andi he'd always known was back, warm and friendly… if much more vulnerable than she'd been, and he found himself attracted to the whole package.

But it didn't escape his notice that she was skittish about what had happened between them. She'd blushed when she picked Nicky up from his first tutoring session after the football party, and avoided alone time with him without her son present. He respected the boundaries she set up and kept a respectful distance. They were teacher and parent, and that was all there could be.

Soon September turned to October, the weather grew colder, and before he knew it, Halloween was around the corner. The elementary school hosted a grade-wide parade, and the kids got dressed in their costumes midday, the class moms coming in to help. Because of the work involved and the holiday, they also extended an invitation to all the parents who wanted to come see the kids dressed up.

Thanks to the excitement of the holiday, he never expected to get any real work accomplished with the kids, and instead he had a relaxed day planned. The morning went by quickly and soon the parents arrived. It was a hectic jumble of madness, costumes, and loud, excited voices.

Even Andi had taken the afternoon off from her job to be there for Nicky, and it took a concerted effort for Kyle to pay attention to the other parents and children and not focus solely on Andi. He couldn't stop staring at her lush figure in jeans that accentuated her curvy ass and hips, and more than once, he had to jolt himself into awareness and force himself to look away and do his job.

They made it through the costume parade around the school, followed by the class party with cupcakes and sugar highs. As much as he enjoyed the holiday and the enthusiasm of his students, it was a relief when the day ended and the kids began to drift out of the room, accompanied by their parents.

Although Nicky didn't have a tutoring session planned for the afternoon, he seemed to be procrastinating taking his Harry Potter costume off and getting his books together.

Andi shot Kyle a frustrated glance as the boy bent down to tie his sneakers for the second time.

"Mom, I need to go to the bathroom before we leave."

She sighed. "Go. Hurry up. And don't forget to wash your hands," she said as he shuffled to the door. She turned to Kyle. "Reverse sugar high?" she asked. "He's not bouncing off the walls. He's just plain exhausted. And we still have trick-or-treating to get through." She sounded tired herself.

"With a little luck, you'll get a second wind. I like how he chose Harry Potter as his costume. It tells me he's really into the story."

"Oh, he is. And I notice a definite difference in his willingness to sit down and read. Is it translating to his schoolwork? Not as much, but a little," she said, obviously grateful for the slight change.

"Do you remember the Halloween we dressed up as Harry Potter and Hermione?" she asked.

The memory washed over him as if it were yesterday. They'd done everything together, including coordinating their costumes. They would laugh and were completely in sync.

Smiling at the memory, he teased, "You were so insistent that you be Hermione and not Ginny."

"Well, I still think Harry should have ended up with Hermione."

"I know, I know." He shook his head. "Poor Ron."

She grinned.

He missed those days, now more than ever, since they were together in the same room, communicating... kissing. "It was fun back then, wasn't it?"

She nodded, her eyes softening as she looked at him, the memory clearly affecting her, too.

He stepped forward and inhaled her peach-scented shampoo. Reaching out, he tucked a strand of hair behind her ear, the smell arousing him, making him aware of her as a very feminine woman he desired. "We were good together."

As friends. Now they could be more and he suddenly realized how much he wanted that *more*. Heart pounding inside his chest, he skimmed his knuckles down her cheek and she sighed, leaning into him.

His body tightened with need, desire winding its way through him. He didn't have to do more than breathe in her scent and he responded. He leaned in closer, his lips a millimeter from hers.

Noise in the hallway brought them back into the present.

She jerked back, realizing she'd almost been caught in a compromising position. She blushed, ducking her head.

He blew out a harsh breath. He ought to be annoyed with himself. After all, he was the teacher, the one who needed to be a professional while in school. But he couldn't bring himself to regret this tentative reaching out to Andi. He felt the potential between them, the possibilities in the air.

And he made a decision. This time he wasn't going to pull back and give her space.

This time, he was going go after what he wanted.

"I realize this probably isn't the right time…" He paused in thought. "But if I overthink things, no time will be the right time."

She tilted her head and looked into his eyes. "What's going on?" she asked, obviously curious.

"I want to see you. Alone. As in, you and I go out on a date."

"Kyle, I'm really in no position to date anyone."

"I'm not just anyone. How about we say we're just two old friends catching up and start there?"

She laughed at that. "We can't be in the same

room together without acting on this new attraction. I don't think we can go back to just two friends catching up."

"At least you admit to an attraction. Can you really walk away from that? From me... again?" Yeah, he went there.

Because to get what he wanted, he had to push.

She sucked in a shallow breath. "No," she whispered. "I can't. I just can't make any promises."

"One date at a time," he assured her.

She nodded. "Okay." Her soft lips curved upward in a smile, one that he felt in his gut. "Give me your phone and I'll send myself a text. That way you'll have my number."

"And you'll have mine?" she asked, laughing.

He chuckled. "Yeah."

She handed over her iPhone and he input his number, sending her a message for her to look at later.

"Ready, Mom!" Nicky's return ended any personal conversation but Kyle had accomplished his goal.

She'd agreed to a date. And he had a chance to win over the woman he'd always desired.

ANDI WAS ELBOW deep in a floral arrangement, in a good mood she was reluctant to attribute to Kyle Davenport, but how could she not? She hadn't looked at her phone until much later last night, his text causing warm flutters in her stomach.

I waited a lifetime for this date. Let me know what night is good for you.

He made it sound like he'd always had the desire to go out with her, even when they'd been just friends. The thought was overwhelming. She'd meant it when she said she was in no position to date. She was a full-time mom, a full-time worker, and a woman with a past that made her wary of a future with any man. Even one she ought to be able to trust. But she could go out with him and catch up. She could enjoy herself a little. She deserved at least that, didn't she?

She texted him back that she could see him Friday night, when Nicky went to Kane and Halley's for an overnight. Then she began to obsess about what to wear, wondering where they were going and generally acting like a teenager going on a first date. She figured she'd ask him where they were going tonight when she picked Nicky up from his tutoring session.

She was lost in thought when her cell phone rang. "Andi? It's Rhonda Sharpe," an old classmate said.

"Rhonda, how are you?" Andi asked.

"I'm good, thanks. But I'm calling with news. Francine Gray was brought into the hospital earlier," Rhonda said, and Andi recalled the other woman was a social worker at the local hospital.

Andi gripped the phone tighter. "Is she okay?"

"I'm sorry, but she passed away. Your number was under her in-case-of-emergency contact, so I thought I should call you."

Shock followed by a deep sadness enveloped her at the news. She placed the scissors down and lowered herself into the nearest chair. "What happened?"

"An aneurism," Rhonda said. "She didn't suffer."

Andi drew a deep breath and didn't reply, relieved for Francine, yet sad at the same time.

"Andi, are you okay?" Rhonda asked in the wake of her silence.

"I'm just in shock. Thanks for letting me know."

Her hands shook and a tear dripped down her face. She'd been fond of Francine, and she saw her monthly, after all. If Billy hadn't always been between them, a presence even once he had left town, they might have been closer. Now she was gone.

And she had to tell her son he'd lost his grand-mother.

She washed her face and pulled herself together before leaving the store in capable hands and heading over to school to pick him up early. Although there was slim chance he'd hear the news, she didn't want to worry that someone else might tell him what she needed to handle herself.

The last school bell went off and she walked to the

classroom. Kyle and Nicky were talking quietly, a book open between them.

"Hi," she said, interrupting them.

"Hey there." Kyle's welcoming grin caused flutters in her stomach. Flutters that were becoming increasingly familiar each time she so much as thought of Kyle.

"Mom! Is it time to go already?" Nicky asked, sounding disappointed.

"Yeah, kiddo. Something's come up." She glanced at Kyle before turning to her son. "Can you go get your things together?"

He picked up his book and rushed over to his backpack, hanging on a hook on the back wall.

"Billy's mom passed away," she said quietly. "I wanted to take Nicky home and explain things to him before he heard it somewhere else."

"I'm sorry," he said. "I'm sure it's not easy."

She nodded. "I liked her but we weren't close because of Billy. She couldn't quite bring herself to see her son as a villain." She shuddered at the thought of her ex-husband.

As if sensing her reaction and why, Kyle reached out and placed a reassuring hand on her shoulder. "It's in your past."

She nodded. She hoped so, but with Francine gone, she was afraid Billy would return to claim whatever her inheritance consisted of. She grew nauseous at the thought.

"Kyle, I'm going to have to cancel tonight," she said, regret in her voice. "Nicky might need me."

"Of course." He clasped her hand in his, squeezing for reassurance.

His warmth trickled through her.

"What if I picked up dinner and brought it over? Or is that too… presumptuous?" he asked.

She thought about it and nodded. "That would be nice," she said. "It will help break up his night." And hers.

She appreciated his willingness to change plans and step up to help. She didn't know how Nicky would react to losing his grandmother. Their relationship had been strained, her wanting to talk about Billy, neither Andi nor Nicky desiring the same.

Telling Nicky was difficult. It was his first experience with death, but he was old enough to understand his grandma was gone. He didn't cry, which concerned her, and she was determined to keep an eye on him and make sure he was dealing with the loss and processing his feelings in a healthy way.

"Mom? Can I go to my room?" he asked.

She ruffled his hair and nodded. "If you need me, you know where to find me." She'd already called Kane and Halley to cancel his visit tonight. She wanted him home in his own bed.

"I know." He rose from his seat.

"Hey, Mr. Davenport is coming by with dinner," she said, hoping the news would perk him up a bit.

"Cool." Shoulders still slumped, he headed for his bedroom.

Not even the fact that his favorite teacher would be visiting had helped him smile and she understood. She let him go, knowing he both needed and deserved time alone.

She set the table for dinner and then headed to the bedroom to freshen up before Kyle arrived. She'd had sad news and shouldn't be focused on how she looked, but she couldn't deny that she cared how he viewed her. He always saw her at the end of the day, rushing from work to pick up Nicky, and this was her chance to look good for him.

She splashed cold water on her face, wiping away the evidence of her earlier tears for Francine, and reapplied her makeup. She took a quick shower, getting out of the dirt-stained jeans from work and into a fresh pair of denim, along with a mauve-colored top that outlined her curves.

She'd come to accept the fact that something was brewing between them that she couldn't ignore and didn't want to. It didn't have to make her nervous, not if he understood what she was able to share of herself going into the relationship. The thought of giving herself to another man in any capacity – be it physically or emotionally – was scary for so many reasons, but this was Kyle. If anyone wouldn't hurt her, it was him. And he was also capable of understanding she was keeping her heart under lock and key from now on. Only she was in control of her destiny.

But she was getting ahead of herself. All he was asking for was a date. She could take things one day at a time and enjoy him.

That was the thought in her head when the doorbell rang and she walked over to let him inside. He carried brown bags filled with delicious-smelling food.

"What have you got there?" she asked as she let him inside.

"I stopped by the new Italian place in town and picked up your favorite. Well, what I remembered was your favorite. Chicken parmigiana and lasagna for Nicky. I figured I couldn't go wrong there."

She grinned, pleased he remembered the food she liked best, recalling times his mother had cooked the dish just because she'd known Andi liked it and was coming for dinner. "Thank you. Come on in. I'll put all this in the kitchen." She tried to take the bags from him but he insisted on carrying them into the other room.

Placing the food on the counter, he turned to face

her. His scruff had grown in over the course of the day, making him look even sexier than usual, and she squirmed in her jeans, because she couldn't stop thinking about what the light beard would feel like rubbing against her skin.

"How did Nicky take the news?" Kyle asked.

She shook her head. "I'm honestly not sure. He didn't have much to say about it. He nodded a lot, said he understood, and asked to go to his room. I figured he needed time to process. I'm hoping he'll be more himself at dinner."

"Death is hard for adults to comprehend, then we have to explain it to kids. He'll be okay because he has you. He knows you're there for him."

"Thank you. I needed to hear that."

"Why don't you go get him and I'll put the food out on the table."

But when she stopped at Nicky's room and glanced inside, he'd fallen asleep, his *Harry Potter* book open beside him. He'd had a long, trying day and she decided to let him be. She tiptoed inside, moved the book, and put it on the nightstand.

She watched for a few minutes, his chest rising and falling with the even cadence of his breathing. She smiled and walked quietly out of the room, shutting the door softly behind her.

"Where is he?" Kyle asked as she reentered the

kitchen.

"Out like a light. I didn't want to wake him. He can get something to eat when he wakes up. Or in the morning if he really crashes for that long."

"So it's just us?" he asked in a gruff voice.

"It is." A smile teased the edges of her mouth. She was feeling more herself around him than she had since his return.

She glanced at the table, open tins of food just waiting for them to eat. "Oh look! You really got everything out and ready. Thank you."

"Not a problem."

They settled into seats and she served them each a portion of the chicken and lasagna, wrapping up food for Nicky to eat later. While they ate, they talked about his year at school so far and what it was like to be home again. But after they'd cleaned up together and she made them coffee, they moved to the family room, sitting side by side on the couch.

"So tell me about your life before you returned. Did you like living in Illinois?" she asked, lifting the mug of coffee to her lips.

He met her gaze, a serious expression on his face. "It was good to get away. To be honest, I couldn't be here after you cut ties. The shock, the hurt… It was all too much. I didn't want to watch you living your life here without me in it."

She burned her tongue at the same time he answered, and she lowered the cup, placing it on the table in front of the sofa. At his honest words, pain lanced through her, reminding her of the time she'd actually had to do it. Let him go in order to protect him. When she'd asked the question, she hadn't anticipated going *there*, but she supposed if they were really going to get past it, they'd have to talk about it sometime.

"I had my reasons for what I did." She bit down on her lower lip to stop the trembling. "In the beginning, Billy was the charming guy everyone saw at school. It was only later, once I'd really gotten involved with him, that he became possessive. And he hated our relationship. He was jealous of you and he never missed a chance to let me know it."

"Why didn't you walk away?" he asked, jaw clenched, his disdain for her ex obvious.

For all Billy's earlier charm, Kyle had never been fooled. He'd seen through him from the beginning, had tried to warn her not to get involved. But when the star quarterback had turned his attention her way, she'd had stars in her eyes and was flattered someone with his popularity would be interested in her.

"Early on, his mild jealousy was flattering. I didn't take it all that seriously. By the time I realized what I was dealing with, I couldn't just leave."

"Because you were afraid?" he asked, jaw clenched, his gaze too knowing.

"What makes you say that?" She didn't discuss this. With anyone.

"Really? You're going to play dumb with me? Even after all these years, you know you can tell me anything." He paused. "Or maybe not considering I didn't know a damn thing before you cut off our friendship completely."

She swallowed hard. "Fine. You want the truth? I ended our friendship to protect you. Because he told me if I didn't stop talking to you, he'd hurt you, and by then I knew enough about his temper and actions to believe him."

The truth stopped him cold, his eyes opening wide, fists clenching at his sides. "Holy shit, Andi. And you didn't think to tell me this? To let me help you get out of the situation before you married him?"

She blinked, the angry tone in his voice hurtling through her, and she backed away, into the comfort and safety of the side arm of the couch. "I was pregnant by then," she whispered.

She'd had no choice but to go along with what he wanted. She couldn't have made the pregnancy Kane's problem. He'd taken care of them after their mom died, when their dad was out gambling instead of being home with his family. She'd known she had to deal with the consequences of her actions.

"I'm sorry." He raised his hands in a gesture of peace. "I'm just frustrated," he said, his voice softening along with his expression. "All these years lost. All the years of me thinking you just turned your back on me." He shook his head and relaxed his shoulders.

"He'd have gone after you. I know it." And she did. With everything in her being, she believed she'd done the right thing.

He slowly eased in closer, taking his time, no sudden movements, as he picked her hand up and held it tight in his. "I could have taken care of myself. I would have taken care of you."

Their eyes met. Locked. Both knew they couldn't change the past. She knew that past defined her present and future. Only she would be in charge of her destiny from here on out. No man would tell her what to do ever again. But none of that erased the desire racing between them. Wanting him didn't mean she was giving up the part of herself she'd reclaimed. She could indulge in something temporary without worrying about permanent attachments.

She cupped his face in her hand. "Can't we leave the past where it belongs?"

"If it means I can have you now, then yes." He dipped his head, his lips coming down on hers.

He kissed her hard, the chemistry between them

incredible. His lips slid over hers, mouths parting, tongues gliding, teeth clashing, each unable to get enough. Desire hit her hard, her nipples hardening beneath her shirt, wetness pooling between her thighs.

How long had it been since she reacted to a man? Just Kyle, and before him, she'd thought that part of her had died. She welcomed the renewal of feelings and slid her fingers into his hair, holding his head close to hers as he feasted on her mouth, his tongue doing delicious things to hers.

"Can't get enough," he said as he came up for air before diving into her once more, easing her back against the arm of the sofa.

He came down over her. Lifting her shirt, he glided his hand upward, fingertips skimming along her rib cage, his big hand cupping her breast. He slid his thumb over her nipple and she writhed beneath him, the sensations traveling straight to her core. She couldn't remain still, arching her back and pushing her sex against the ridge of his erection, which had settled between her legs.

Hard and rigid, his thickness ground against her most sensitive spot, causing sparks to dance behind her eyes. "Mmm." She moaned at the intimate contact, knowing if she kept it up, she'd come, but he lifted himself off her, rolling to the side.

"Why are you stopping?"

"Because I need to touch you." He unbuttoned then unzipped her jeans, easing his hand into the waistband, his fingers trailing over the wetness in her panties. Edging the jeans down enough to make room, he pushed aside the silk material and slid a hand over her soaked sex, her body trembling in response to the glide of his fingers.

She arched into him, seeking more of his touch, more of the sensations growing inside her. He slicked a finger over her clit and a wash of arousal followed, her hips rolling as she chased the feeling. He kept up the pressure until the orgasm swept through her and she soared. She would have yelled out loud except Kyle anticipated the moment and sealed his lips over hers, swallowing the sound.

She trembled, coming down from the high of her climax, falling lax against the couch. She opened her eyes to find his intense gaze studying her face. Reaching out, she brushed a hand over the hard ridge of his erection.

He shook his head, grasping her wrist. "That was about you." He helped her pull up and refasten her jeans. "What happens next is about us."

She knew he wasn't talking about just sex. "I want to spend more time with you. I just can't make any promises about the future."

"No worries," he assured her. "We're on the same

page. Make time for me in your life and I have what I want."

She blew out a relieved breath and smiled. She could handle that. She wanted him in her life again. "Okay."

"Okay." He pulled her to a sitting position, a satisfied grin on his handsome face. "Now when can I see you again?" he asked, obviously pressing his advantage.

"I'll let you know the next time Nicky's going to a sleepover or when my brother is watching him. He should ask for a makeup for tonight once he's feeling better."

"Good." He braced his hands on his thighs. "I hate to bring it up, but will you have to get through a funeral for your ex-mother-in-law?"

She shook her head. "She once told me she would want a small graveside funeral. I'm not family anymore and I'm not going to put Nicky through that. Especially since there's always a chance his father will show up." She ran her hands over the goose bumps that had risen on the flesh on her arms at the thought, which wasn't far from possible.

"You aren't alone this time, right?" He met her gaze, his stare warm and steady.

But she'd always be alone. She'd come to accept that reality as the only way she could be in charge of her own life.

Still, she understood his point. "I know." Not that she'd inflict Billy on Kyle now any more than she would have in the past, but she wasn't about to argue with him.

She'd learned a lot since her divorce, since she'd been the young girl who'd let him abuse her. Was she still afraid? Yes. Would she protect Billy and keep his actions to herself? Never again.

But she didn't intend to let him take up any of her present, not unless she was faced with him again. So she looked up at Kyle and cupped his face in her hand. "I just want to enjoy the here and now. I want to enjoy you."

"Amen to that," he said, leaning in and brushing his lips across hers.

Chapter Five

A NDI'S NEXT CHANCE to see Kyle came sooner than she'd expected. Kane called her the following week, offering to take Nicky to the city for a Saturday night game at Yankee Stadium, where the team was playing his favorite Boston Red Sox. Unfortunately, when she called Kyle to tell him that she was free that night, he already had plans to go to the Blue Wall with Ryan Mueller. As luck would have it, Georgia's husband was out of town, and she later asked Andi to go out that same evening. Andi suggested the Blue Wall, knowing that would let her meet up with Kyle and surprise him there.

It had been a long time since she'd prepared to be with a man but tonight she wasn't taking any chances. She showered and shaved her legs, washing with her favorite peach-scented wash, followed by a complementary moisturizer. She rubbed the cream up and down her arms and legs, softening her skin. Even over a week later, her body was still tingling at the memory of the orgasm Kyle had given her, the craving to be closer to him growing with each passing day.

Georgia offered to drive and Andi let her, knowing this way she could have a drink or two if she desired or decide to leave and spend the night with Kyle, something she had been contemplating doing all week. Knowing they were on the same page with expectations made it easier for her to let go and be with him sexually, because he wouldn't want anything emotional from her in return. She just didn't think she had it in her to give, not when she was so intent on being independent and self-reliant. And he seemed to understand.

At the thought of being with Kyle again, her nipples puckered beneath the camisole she wore. She blew out a long breath and slipped on a lightweight V-neck sweater, giving her the option to take if off if it was warm in the bar. She paired it with tight jeans and high boots.

One last glance in the mirror and she decided she liked the way she looked. She fluffed out her hair and repaired her lip gloss before heading to the door to wait for her ride.

The Blue Wall was the town's main evening location, a nice restaurant on one side and an upscale bar on the other. Having worked as a hostess for a long time, Andi was more than familiar with the inner workings of the restaurant, but she had rarely gone to the bar for fun.

She arrived to find the place as busy as she'd expect on a Saturday night and butterflies jumped in her stomach as they entered.

"It's a rare night that I go out without my husband," Georgia said as they wove their way through the crowd.

"It's a rare night that I go out," Andi said wryly, and she was excited to be here tonight, to be a woman and not a mom, to flirt and to just enjoy. If she could find the man she was looking for.

"What do you want to drink?" Georgia asked as she reached the bar.

"A white wine spritzer."

"Oh! I'll have the same thing." Georgia turned to place their orders and Andi looked around, not seeing Kyle yet. She swallowed her disappointment and waited for Georgia to turn around with their drinks. Andi figured she would pay for the next round.

With all the people surrounding her, she grew warm and slipped the crocheted sweater over her head, draping it across one arm. She fixed the camisole so it lay correctly, just as Georgia handed her a glass.

"Thanks."

Together they eased forward and finally found an empty place to hang out. Andi took a sip of her bubbly liquid.

"So you mentioned Kyle Davenport came over for

dinner last week. Do tell." Georgia tucked a strand of her wavy blonde hair behind her ear and leaned closer to hear better over the noise of the bar.

Andi figured the heated flush staining her cheeks would answer her friend's question but she replied anyway. "We were best friends as kids but things are more heated between us now," she admitted.

"Oh my God! You are never interested in men! You refuse to let me set you up with anyone, so this must really mean something!"

Andi immediately shook her head. "It can't be serious," she told her friend. "We're just getting to know each other again and maybe crossing new lines. But I'm a mom and I have to focus on myself and my son."

She glanced over to see her friend eyeing her with a speculative gaze. "We'll see. At least you're taking that first step. You deserve to have someone good in your life. I, for one, am happy for you."

Andi smiled. "Thank you," she said, determined to leave it at that.

"Ladies." A blond-haired man she'd never seen before stepped up beside them. "What are two beautiful women like you doing standing all alone?"

Georgia met Andi's gaze and Andi shook her head in response.

Georgia flashed her wedding ring at the man. "Sorry. I'm taken."

"And so is she," a familiar male voice said, and before Andi could react, Kyle stepped between her and the stranger, slipping an arm around her waist. The warmth of his body and the musky scent of his cologne penetrated her senses and she leaned into him, only too happy to let him drive the man off.

The stranger got the message immediately and drifted on to the next group of single women he could find.

"My hero," Andi teased him. "Thanks for saving me."

He met her gaze, his golden-brown gaze hot and intense as he focused on her. "I'm not letting another man come near you when it's taken me this long to get my hands on you."

"Aww, look at you two." Georgia held up her drink in a toast of approval. She made a show of glancing around before saying, "I see someone I need to talk to. I'll catch up with you later, Andi. Bye, Kyle." She not-so-subtly waved her free hand and left them alone.

"Well." He met her gaze. "This is a nice surprise," he said to her.

She rolled her shoulders but didn't pull out of his embrace, liking the feel of his arm around her. "I thought you might like it. When Georgia said she wanted to go out, I suggested we come here."

He slid a hand over her hip and cupped her possessively against him. "Looking for me?" he asked.

She turned her face upward, taking in his sexy razor stubble and strong jaw. "Maybe I was."

"Then lucky me. Can I get you another drink?" he asked.

"No, I'm still good with this one."

He stepped back and let his gaze roam over her, eyes darkening appreciatively. "Looking good, Ms. Harmon."

She straightened her shoulders, pleased with both his sexual perusal and the fact that he liked what he saw. "Why, thank you, Mr. Davenport." She deliberately fluttered her lashes and he grinned.

Without warning, a shiver took hold and she glanced over her shoulder, feeling like someone was watching her. She looked around, narrowing her gaze on a familiar-looking man who disappeared behind the wall to the restrooms. She shook her head. He merely reminded her of Billy, that was all. She was just being paranoid.

"Is something wrong?" Kyle asked, recapturing her attention.

"Not a thing." She managed a smile. She wasn't about to let anything ruin their night together. "Do you have to get back to Ryan?"

He looked to the bar area and she followed his gaze to see that his friend had caught up with his girlfriend.

"Nope. He's doing just fine on his own."

"Good." Then they had time together and she didn't intend to waste it.

KYLE HAD BEEN holding on to his beer and talking to Ryan about his friend's most recent civil litigation case when he caught sight of Andi and her friend Georgia, chatting on the far side of the bar. He was content to watch, his body stirring at the sight of her relaxed and happy, sipping what looked like wine and smiling at her friend. Until a guy approached them with an interested gleam in his eye.

Then Kyle knew he had to step in, his alpha instincts taking over, everything inside him screaming she was *his*. He knew better than to mention it to her, considering her skittishness about the word *relationship* and how insistent she was about keeping things light and easy. He could do that for her, all the while drawing her in deeper. At least that was his plan.

He'd interrupted them and she didn't seem upset; in fact, she'd said she'd come here knowing she'd find him. They'd just agreed Ryan was fine on his own when a slow song began to play through the speakers and he glanced over at the small dance floor, where a handful of people swayed to the music.

"Join me?" he asked her, extending a hand.

She clasped her fingers inside his, curling them around him. "Sure thing."

They placed their drinks down and he led her to the wooden floor and pulled her into his arms. Tucking her against his chest, he clasped her hand tight and twirled her around in time to the music. The floor grew crowded and they were crunched together, their movements slowing. Not that he minded, the press of their bodies feeling natural and right, building the growing desire between them.

"I never envisioned us together like this," she said as they moved, their hips shifting in synchronicity.

His heart thudded inside his chest as they talked about the one thing he'd kept to himself all these years. "I imagined it. I just never thought my wish would come true."

"You did? You thought of us as more than friends, even back when we were younger?" she asked, clearly stunned by his admission.

He nodded and his body throbbed in agreement, the yearning he'd had for her a familiar feeling except now it was closer to fulfillment. "I was just too young, too scared to tell you the truth. And then time ran out."

"Billy," she said, a full-body shudder taking hold.

He wrapped her tighter in his arms. "Not a name we're going to let come between us tonight."

Or ever.

She smiled at his words, her face lighting up in agreement. "I like how you think." Her gaze locked on his and he lowered his head, his lips meeting hers.

He stopped dancing, his sole focus on her mouth, kissing her and letting her know without words how quickly he was falling. Or he should say falling all over again, this time for real, because he was getting the chance to explore all facets of her, including the desire he'd never been able to express before.

He slid his hands around her waist, his fingertips gliding down to her ass, and he held her closer. Need pulsed through him, his cock hard in his pants, and he knew he couldn't stay in public any longer.

"Want to get out of here?" And so she couldn't mistake his meaning, he ground himself into the cradle of her legs, his groin surrounded by warmth and heat.

When her eyes darkened, he read the same desire there that was pounding inside of him and she nodded.

"My place," he said, sliding his hand into hers.

"Yes."

On the way out, she stopped to let Georgia know she was leaving with him and wouldn't need a ride home, and then he helped her into his car. The sedan was new, something he'd bought when he returned home, and usually he noticed the new-car smell, but when he came around the driver's side and climbed in, her scent overtook him, the intoxicating fruity smell permeating his skin and his senses.

He gripped the steering wheel harder, the drive to his place a test of his patience and ability to control himself when all he wanted to do was pull over to the side of the road, yank Andi onto his lap, and thrust deep inside her.

He swallowed hard and decided to be sure they were on the same page. "Second thoughts?" he asked, giving her an out.

In reply, she inched her fingers across the center console and placed a hand on his thigh, the contact burning his skin through the denim, and squeezed his leg, her fingers pressing deep. "Not at all. In fact, I was just wondering if you could drive faster." The corners of her lips lifted in a sexy smile.

He had his answer.

A few sexual-tension-filled minutes later, he pulled into the driveway of his house and tapped the electric garage door opener so he could drive inside. He cut the engine and came around to her side of the car, then helped her out.

His hand on the small of her back, his heart

pounding inside his chest, he led her into the house he'd bought never thinking Andi would step inside and shut the door behind them.

He walked them into the kitchen and dropped the keys in a bowl, then turned and pulled her into his arms. She met him halfway and their mouths joined. Melded. Their bodies came together as if they couldn't get to each other fast enough.

His tongue slid between her lips, devouring her, sliding back and forth, only breaking the kiss when he couldn't wait to get his hands on her bare skin.

"Bedroom," he said, grasping her hand and leading her to his room in the back of the house, where the light of the lamp he'd left on guided the way.

No sooner did he have her beside the bed than they came together again, their lips colliding, tongues tangling, fingers fisting in each other's hair. He'd never brought a woman to this place, no one in Rosewood Bay interesting him enough to get this far in the short time he'd been back. Andi was different. She always had been.

She broke the kiss and placed her hands on the hem of his shirt, pulling it up and over his head. Her hands slid up his abdomen, her fingers gliding along his skin, causing an electric current to run along his nerve endings.

"I don't remember you being so fit," she murmured, obviously pleased with what she saw and felt beneath her palms.

"I work out," he said.

"It shows and I like it." She skimmed her nails over his nipples and his cock jerked in response.

Grasping her wrists, he pulled her hands away from his body and pulled them to her sides and out of the way. "I'm glad. But I want to focus on you." He wanted to see her come apart beneath his mouth, his fingers, and then when he was inside her soft, wet body.

"You've done that once," she said, cheeks flushing.

Not that he needed reminding. The feel of her slick wetness beneath his fingertips was never far from his mind and he wanted to feel her again now.

He also wanted to see her in all her naked glory. "And I'm going to do it again. Let's get you undressed."

Before he could reach out, she kicked off her sandals and stripped off her shirt, leaving her in a bra and jeans, revealing the swells of her breasts pushing upward from the cups of her bra. She reached behind her and removed the flimsy garment next and his mouth ran dry and his cock strained against his pants at the sight of her bared before him.

Her gaze never leaving his, she unbuttoned her jeans, hooked her fingers into the waistband, and pulled them, along with her panties, down and off her long legs.

This Andi, the siren with her brown hair flowing over her shoulders, was everything he'd dreamed about as she faced him, glorious in her nudity.

"Now it's your turn," she said, her gaze on the bulging strain of his erection.

He had no problem reciprocating and immediately undressed, tossing his clothes into a pile on the floor.

ANDI STOOD BEFORE Kyle, her nipples puckering thanks to the cool air and his hot gaze. And when he stripped, revealing the hard male body she'd only envisioned before, her underused hormones went into overdrive.

"I dreamed of this," he said, his words washing over her, causing wetness to drip between her thighs. "I dreamed of you." He lifted her chin in his hand and his lips came down on hers. Flames immediately consumed her, desire sweeping through her like wildfire.

Next thing she knew, he pressed her back against the mattress, his big, hard body coming down over hers. She sighed at the feel of his warmth, groaned at the strength of the erection grinding into her sex. She ran a foot up his hair-roughened calf, closing her eyes at the feel of him on top of her.

They worked their way to the head of the bed and he rose to straddle her, his cock sliding along her damp sex. From a sitting position, he cupped her breasts in his hands, rolling her nipples back and forth between his thumbs and forefingers. She arched into him, the sensations he created causing arousal to streak through her, from her breasts to her clit, desire a living, breathing thing inside her.

He stared down at her almost reverently as he slid a hand down her stomach, his fingers taking a path south, cupping her in his hand. "I'm going to make you come," he promised, easing his big body downward so his face was level with her sex.

Without waiting, he slid his tongue over her clit, back and forth, teasing her mercilessly. She moaned and writhed beneath him, but he was determined and didn't let up, his hands on her thighs, his mouth devouring her, lapping at where she needed him most. It didn't take long for him to bring her up and over, a quick but thorough and explosive climax startling her in its intensity.

She relaxed afterwards, lax against the bed, and when she opened her eyes, his face was level with hers, a satisfied gleam in his golden-brown eyes. "That was just the beginning," he said, his tone a promise.

He slid his lips over hers and she tasted herself on

him, surprised by the intimacy of the act. His cock pressed hard and insistently against her and she moaned, arching herself up, shocked to discover waves of desire alive inside her once more.

He broke the kiss and stared down at her for a moment, his eyes soft before he pulled back. "Condom," he muttered, reaching over and opening his nightstand drawer.

As she watched, he ripped open a foil packet and slid protection over his thick, straining erection. She swallowed hard, knowing how long it had been since she'd had sex. Since she'd allowed any man the privilege of entry into her body or allowed herself the pleasure. In fact, she couldn't remember the last time sex had equaled pleasure.

But everything with Kyle was all of that and more. He focused on her, also a first for her. Now it was their turn together.

He aligned himself at her entrance. She was wet and ready, she knew, and though he slid into her easily at first, she was tight and he paused before thrusting inside. She gasped, feeling her body soften and adjust, and almost immediately, she felt a quickening that had her tightening herself around him.

"Damn, that feels good. Do it again."

With a grin, she squeezed her inner muscles and he let out a low groan that vibrated through his body and affected hers.

"Yeah, like that." He braced his hands on either side of her shoulders and glided out of her, then thrust back in deep, the sheer width and length of him causing shudders all through her.

She gripped his shoulders, her nails digging into his skin as he began a steady glide, lifting her hips as he pumped in and out, filling her up. And with each successive collision of their bodies, she soared higher, sensations gathering low in her belly and building, growing stronger and more powerful.

He slipped a hand between their bodies, his fingertip gliding back and forth over her clit, pressing down as the first tremor hit.

"Oh God." She moaned and he began to rub harder, holding her in place as he played with her clit until the sensations became overwhelming and she bucked against him, nipping at his shoulder as she came, stars sparkling behind her eyes, warmth and beautiful sensation filling her.

Suddenly he groaned, removed his hand, braced himself, and began to pound his body into hers, immediately hitting the right spot, as if he knew her intimately already. She felt him inside her, staking his claim, marking her indelibly, showing her a side of sex she hadn't known existed.

Over and over he slammed into her, and each time

she came closer to another climax. It didn't take long for a second orgasm to take hold, her body flying, the sensations unlike anything she'd felt before. As if he'd waited for her and now had permission, he stilled, his big body shaking above her as he followed her over the edge.

He pushed himself to the side, collapsing beside her, his body warm and hard where it aligned with hers. After a few silent minutes when they each caught their breath, he rolled to his side, facing her.

"Okay?" he asked, brushing a strand of hair off her face.

"Yeah. I'm good." She bit down on the inside of her cheek before admitting, "Better than good. I'm great."

He studied her with his intense gaze, prompting her to continue.

"It's just… I'm not used to someone taking care of me first. And during. It was an enlightening experience." Despite the intensity of the conversation, she felt comfortable admitting these truths to Kyle.

His face hardened at the admission. "That's a damned shame. You should always come… first, second, and during," he said, his expression softening thanks to a teasing grin lifting his lips.

She laughed, appreciating his attempt at lightening the conversation.

"Hang on. I'll be right back."

In the silent moments that followed, while he disappeared into the bathroom, she wondered if she should get dressed and go. She wanted to keep this casual and she had no business assuming he'd want her to stay longer.

She rolled toward the edge, and he stepped out of the bathroom just as she was lowering her legs to the floor.

He walked out, his naked body a sight to behold, and slid back onto the bed, pushing himself to her side. His arm snaked out and yanked her back. "Where do you think you're going?" he asked.

"Home?" It came out as a question instead of an answer.

"Nope. Unless you have to get back for Nicky?" he asked.

She shook her head. "He's at my brother's, but…"

"No buts. You're staying. Who knows when we'll have another night alone."

Her shoulders relaxed as she released a breath she hadn't been aware of holding. She couldn't argue with his reasoning nor could she deny the fact that she wanted to stay here with him.

"Okay," she said.

He pulled her to him, slid a leg over hers, and they rolled together into a comfortable position on the bed.

"Hang on." He reached over to his side and shut off the lamp.

She closed her eyes, his body solid and sure against hers. She breathed in and out, reassuring herself that just because she spent the night with Kyle didn't mean she was getting in too deep.

✧　✧　✧

ANDI WOKE UP alone in an unfamiliar bed. She stretched, awareness coming to her as she remembered she'd stayed with Kyle. After having slept with him. More than once, since they'd woken up in the middle of the night and shared sleepy sex that had been incredible and felt more intimate than the first time.

The slow way he'd entered her, the easy glide of his body in and out of hers. The warmth of his hands on her breasts, his mouth on her lips. She shivered at the memory, her nipples puckering and her body softening, as she wished he was in bed with her now. Instead she climbed off the mattress and headed for the bathroom to wash up. She noticed he'd left her a towel and she took a much-needed shower, getting lost in the musky scent of his body wash, another reminder of the night they'd shared.

She dressed in last night's clothes, stretched-out jeans, her top, and the sweater, and headed downstairs, where she heard noises from the kitchen. As she came closer, she smelled something delicious cooking and her stomach grumbled loudly.

She stepped into the room and the sight she viewed took her breath away. Kyle stood in front of the stove, wearing a pair of faded jeans and nothing else. Bare feet peeked out from beneath the hems and muscles flexed in his back as he worked at the stove, spatula in hand.

She swallowed hard. "Smells delicious. What are you cooking?" she asked, stepping into the small but obviously newly renovated kitchen.

"French toast."

"Oh wow. That's quite the treat."

"I figured you don't get a chance to have someone cook for you." He glanced over his shoulder and treated her to a sexy smile, causing her stomach to tumble over with warmth and sexual desire.

"Thank you," she said in a hoarse voice.

"My pleasure." He turned back to the stove in time to flip the cooked bread off the frying pan and onto a plate. "Ready. Can you grab the syrup from the fridge?"

"Sure." She took out the maple syrup along with the orange juice and placed them on the table, while he grabbed glasses and silverware, then joined her.

She had to move aside what looked like exam papers with a red pen on top to make room for them to eat. She glanced at the red pen and grinned, remembering something from their teenage years. "What happened to the guy who hated red ink?"

To Kyle, the red had always represented mistakes and failure. He'd disliked how the color called attention to his errors.

He laughed. "He grew up and became a teacher."

"A good, caring teacher." She put a forkful of French toast into her mouth and moaned at the delicious taste.

At the sound, his gaze shot to hers.

"You're also a great cook."

He grinned. "I just like to eat and I didn't want to spend every meal at a restaurant, so I taught myself."

He could make her come and fuck her like a rock star, as well as cook. He really was a keeper, she mused, then pushed aside the thought. "Well, I'm impressed. I do the best I can to feed Nicky and me." She shrugged. "So far he hasn't complained."

Kyle folded his arms in front of him on the table. "You'll have to feed me sometime so I can see for myself."

She blinked in surprise. "Was that a request for an invite?" she asked.

He met her gaze with an intent one of his own. "Would you extend me one?"

At this point she was afraid she'd let him have anything he asked for. She popped another piece of French toast into her mouth and merely grinned. No need to let him know how much he was getting to her. When they were finished eating, she wiped her mouth and put the napkin on the table.

"I really need to pick up Nicky from my brother's," she said after she had helped him clean up. She wiped her hands on a dish towel.

He walked her to the bedroom to collect her purse, and before she could say goodbye and walk out, he spun her around, pulled her into his arms, and sealed his lips over hers. She moaned, reservations about how serious she was feeling about him slipping away in the wake of his kiss.

He tasted syrupy sweet with a hint of cinnamon and she dove in for more, their tongues mating, her fingers threading through his hair and holding on as he assaulted her mouth. He obviously wasn't letting her leave without a thorough goodbye and she couldn't bring herself to mind.

He slid his hands into the back pockets of her jeans and hauled her against him, his cock thick and hard against her sex.

He lifted his head from hers and took a deep breath. "If I have to let you go, I need to get my fill," he said, and dove into her once more. His lips were hard and demanding against hers while he ground himself against her, want building inside her.

Before she knew what was happening, he stepped back. "There," he said, his lips wet from their kiss. "You'll definitely remember how good we are together," he said, sounding satisfied. "Now let me drive you back to your place."

Dazed from the sensual assault, she still managed to recall suddenly that she didn't have her car here and that she needed to change into fresh clothes so she didn't roll into her brother's house doing the walk of shame. Not that she was ashamed of what she did with Kyle.

She was just overwhelmed and worried that she could fall for him hard at a time when she needed to stand on her own two feet.

Chapter Six

ANDI WAS SURPRISED when Phoebe called and asked her to make time in her busy schedule for a quick lunch. Knowing her friend wouldn't ask her to take time from work unless it was important, Andi requested that one of her employees cover the shop and met Phoebe at Grace's Coffee Shop in town.

She walked into the familiar restaurant and saw Phoebe's white-blonde hair in the back corner. Andi joined her, sliding into a booth.

"Hi," she said, putting her purse down next to her.

"Hi, yourself. Thanks for meeting me."

Andi glanced at Phoebe, dressed in a cream-colored suit, her hair in a twist, looking like she'd come from a Realtor appointment. She was always the epitome of put together and beautiful.

She was also a good friend. "So what's going on?" Andi asked.

"Let's get some coffee and order lunch. I'd rather enjoy ourselves first."

"Okay then." Andi ordered a chicken salad sandwich, Phoebe a tossed salad, which they ate while talking about their kids, school, their activities, and how busy it was being a working mom.

"How's Jake?" Andi asked.

"The great part about coming home at night is that he's there," Phoebe said, sounding like a happily married woman.

Andi smiled. "I'm truly happy for you."

"What about the rumors I hear about you and Kyle Davenport?"

"Rumors?" Andi asked, surprised.

"Don't look so shocked. It's a small town. People talk. You two seem to be getting closer again. Except a different kind of close than just best friends?" Phoebe folded her arms and leaned forward, blatantly pushing for information.

Andi might not be used to talking about her personal life, but this wasn't something she had to hide. Not like when she'd been with Billy and she'd had to disguise bruises and sadness behind long sleeves and a fake smile.

"Kyle and I… Back when we were kids, we were close. Good friends. If he felt something more, he never let on. If he'd said something, if I'd known he was interested, I might have chosen differently." She shook her head, knowing it did no good to look back. "But now he's confident and he goes after what he wants."

"And he wants you." Phoebe grinned. "You could do a lot worse than a hot teacher," she said, laughing. "And a good man like Kyle."

Andi toyed with the unused fork on the table. "Here's the thing. I'm back on my feet. I have a good life. I can support my son and I don't have a man telling me what to do and when to do it."

"Kyle doesn't strike me as that kind of man," Phoebe said, her eyes sad at Andi's implication.

"I don't think so either. I just need to be independent. I need to know nobody has power over me anymore."

Phoebe blew out a long breath. "Look, in the right kind of relationship, there is no power play. There's just two people looking out for each other, loving each other. You've never had that. But something tells me with Kyle, you could."

Andi swallowed hard. What Phoebe described sounded like heaven. Did she want that for herself? For her son to see a normal, healthy man-woman relationship? Of course she did. And never in a million years did she think Kyle would hurt her or try to tell her what to do or punish her when she didn't listen. But she lived in fear of giving up the cherished independence that had been hard-won.

Before she could respond, Phoebe went on. "And now I have to tell you why I called to meet and I really don't want to. In fact, I'd give anything to get up and walk out before we have this conversation."

Fear raced over Andi and through her veins. "What is it?"

Phoebe reached across the table and grasped Andi's hand. "One of my brokers got a new listing. There's no easy way to say it, so here goes. Billy came in when I was out of the office and he put his mother's house on the market. Which means—"

"He's back in town." The food she'd eaten threatened to come back up and she wished Phoebe hadn't insisted on a meal before imparting this information. "Thank you for telling me." She appreciated the heads-up, although if she'd listened to her instincts, the feeling she'd had last Saturday night at the Blue Wall, she'd have realized she already knew Billy was back.

She blew out a shaky breath. "At least I know."

"You aren't alone this time," Phoebe said. "You have friends who aren't going anywhere. Jake, Kane, and Kyle would love to have a word with the bastard. Make sure he stays away from you."

She shook her head. "No. I have to handle this myself. I can't be afraid of him anymore and he has to know that."

Phoebe shook her head. "You handled it alone last time."

"No, last time I didn't handle it at all. I let him walk all over me. That's not happening this time." She felt her spine stiffen along with her resolve not to let him rule her by fear this time around.

"There's a good chance he won't want anything to do with me. He doesn't want responsibility for his son, and Nicky and I are a package deal." But even as she spoke, she knew she was wishing for the impossible.

Billy got off on threats, and as far as he knew, it was easy to make Andi cower in fear. He wouldn't come back to town and ignore her. She wouldn't be that lucky.

"I need you to promise me that you'll ask for help this time. If things get out of control, you'll tell Kane or Kyle."

"Sure. Yes. I won't put Nicky at risk."

Phoebe narrowed her eyes. "Don't think I'm stupid, Andi. You didn't say you'd take care of yourself."

"Oh, don't worry. I won't let that bastard hurt me again."

WITH THE SPECTER of Billy hanging over her head, Andi went about her daily life. She dropped Nicky off at school, went to work, jumped when the door to the floral shop opened throughout the day, and headed back to the school to pick her son up when his day ended or his tutoring sessions were over. She'd even called Janie Hudson and had lunch with her one day, taking a step toward renewing the friendship.

Kyle gave her space during the day. He worked, so did she, and she didn't hear from him during school hours. So she was surprised to come home and find she had a floral delivery one evening, along with a card. *I know you love flowers, but I didn't want you to have to work to enjoy them.*

She glanced at the colorful bouquet set in a pink-tinted vase from a floral shop the next town over. They were gorgeous and she appreciated the senti-ment, knowing he'd chosen flowers not because they were easy but because they meant something to her personally.

She smiled and sent him a text, thanking him for the beautiful arrangement.

His answer came immediately. *No way they're as beautiful as you.*

Warmth spread through her at his words. The man knew how to get to her on an emotional level and her heart squeezed tight in her chest.

"Mom! I'm starving!" Nicky called from his room.

She gave the flowers one last glance and refocused on the things she needed to do. "A few more minutes!" she called up to him.

They ate dinner, Nicky talking about his science

project and the kids in his class who were his partners. Her son was a happy, well-adjusted boy who had nothing more to worry about than school and friendships and that's just the way she wanted it. He hadn't always been this way. When his father had been in the picture, he'd been a shell of himself, and she didn't ever want to see him that way again.

Part of keeping him healthy was maintaining her own strength. When he finished his homework and turned in for the night, she opened her laptop and began to look for self-defense classes. She wanted to be able to handle herself with Billy if the need arose. Never again did she want to be cowering in front of him.

To her surprise, the Rosewood Bay Police Department offered a free crime-victim prevention class to educate women about realistic options to help them avoid, escape, and survive assaults. The focus was on mental and physical preparedness, giving women techniques to incorporate into their everyday lives that would increase awareness and reduce the risk of becoming a victim. The two-hour class, offered this Saturday, started with an instructional video and progressed into a hands-on self-defense preparation taught by two law enforcement officers.

She didn't have much free time in her life, but she'd make time for this class. She'd make time to take care of herself and her son. If she told her brother why she needed him to take Nicky for the day, he'd go into overprotective mode and that was something she didn't want. He was happy in his life with Halley and their upcoming baby, and he didn't need to worry about his sister. She'd just tell him she had to work on Saturday because an employee needed the day off.

She exhaled and closed the laptop, feeling proactive, like she was doing something for herself. Something to arm herself in case the worst should happen and Billy decided to try and make himself part of her life again. Although she wanted to believe Billy still had another woman in his life and didn't need her to push around, she had no way of knowing if that was true.

Her cell phone rang and she saw Kyle's name. Her stomach jumped in delight. "Hello?"

"Hi, gorgeous," he said, his voice a deep, husky rumble.

She swallowed hard, unable to stop the smile that pulled at her lips at the compliment. "How are you?"

"Good now that I'm talking to you."

She curled her legs beneath her on the sofa, happy to be talking to him, too.

"So listen. I was thinking, how would you and Nicky like to go pumpkin picking this weekend?"

"Oh, I'd love that and I know he would, too." He

was an amazing man, not just asking her out on a date but thinking of her son, as well. She was certain Nicky would want to spend a day with his favorite teacher and she couldn't deny she wanted to do the same thing.

"Great. How's Saturday?" he asked.

She blew out a long breath, disappointed as she realized the day wouldn't work. "Saturday's no good. I … I have to work."

She hated lying to him but she couldn't tell him her plan to go to a self-defense class or the reason behind it any more than she could tell her brother. Kyle would hit the roof if he knew Billy was back in town and she was preparing for a possible confrontation.

"No problem," he said, easygoing as always. "How about Sunday, then?"

"Perfect. I'm looking forward to it. I was thinking the outside of the house needed some decoration for the holiday season."

Orange pumpkins on the front stoop always gave the outside of her home a festive look. She usually picked them up at the supermarket on one of her weekly runs. She hadn't thought to take Nicky to the local pumpkin farm but she should have.

And now she couldn't wait.

"Sounds like a plan. Everything else good?" he asked.

She ran her tongue over her bottom lip. "Everything is great," she said.

And it was. As long as she didn't hear from or see her ex.

SUNDAY DAWNED A crisp fall morning, perfect to spend the day outdoors. Kyle picked up Andi and Nicky and they drove twenty minutes to the farm outside of town where they sold pumpkins, squash, corn, and other seasonal items, including Halloween decorations for indoors and out. Hayrides were also offered, and of course that was the idea Nicky latched onto as soon as they arrived.

"Can we go on the hayride? Look, Peter's here with his parents and they're in line." He pulled at Andi's coat sleeve to keep her attention.

She glanced at Kyle and he nodded, figuring the day was more about Nicky enjoying it than the adults. He was here for the company, and as long as he could enjoy being with Andi and Nicky, he was good with anything.

"Hayride works for me," he said, and they made their way to the bales of hay and the people waiting in line for the tractor to return with the wagon and pick up the next group of people.

Nicky stood with his friend, and Kyle turned to

Andi. "Remember when we used to do this back in high school?" Once he'd gotten his license, they hadn't needed parents to drive them and they'd come every year.

She nodded, a smile on her face. "I got sick one year!" She covered her face, adorably embarrassed by the memory.

"At least you waited until we got off the back of the wagon before you puked."

"Here it is!" Nicky pointed as the tractor returned and the previous group climbed off.

They lifted themselves onto the back of the wagon and everyone found a place to sit, Nicky choosing a spot in the back with his friend. With everyone's focus on the ride, Kyle settled into a corner and pulled Andi alongside him, wrapping an arm around her waist.

She snuggled into him, not resisting his semi-public show of affection. The peachy scent of her hair tickled his nostrils and gave his body the kick he always felt when close to her. As the tractor drove them along the trail, each bump of the ride threw her against him and he held her close, laughter consuming them throughout the ride.

The driver finally pulled back into the parking area and they climbed off the truck, Andi plucking stray pieces of hay off her jacket, a smile on her face.

One of the last ones off the ride, Nicky met up

with them, his grin huge. "Can I go again?" he asked.

"Maybe later. Right now let's go look for some pumpkins for the front steps."

"Can we get some cider then? And a candy apple?"

She nodded and glanced at Kyle, whispering, "No more rides for him. Once was enough. I don't need him eating, then getting sick."

He nodded in agreement. "Especially if he takes after his mother," he said with a grin.

She playfully smacked his arm. "Cut it out. Let's not talk about that anymore."

He chuckled and grasped her hand, following Nicky, who had headed toward the food stands.

"Andi?" She stopped and turned at the sound of her name. Kyle paused with her as a police officer in uniform, who looked about Kyle's age, walked over and joined them.

"Hi, Gary." She glanced at Kyle. "Kyle, this is Officer Gary Madison. Gary, this is Kyle Davenport."

"Nice to meet you," Gary said, shaking Kyle's hand.

"I didn't expect to run into my star student again this weekend." Gary looked at Andi with appreciation in his gaze.

Star student? Kyle narrowed his gaze, wondering what Gary was referring to.

"We're pumpkin picking. What are you doing here

in uniform?" she asked.

He shrugged. "The owner's a friend of mine. I stopped by to say hello."

They talked for a few more minutes while Kyle silently tried to figure out her connection to the police officer. Finally he left them alone, but before Kyle could question her, Nicky came running over asking for money for food.

Because this day was on him, Kyle insisted on paying. He realized he wouldn't have time to talk to her in this crowded atmosphere, so he resigned himself to having fun now and asking questions later.

They drank apple cider, let Nicky have the candy apple that was sticky and got all over his hands and shirt despite his age, picked out pumpkins with faces for Andi's front stoop and plain ones for Kyle's.

He couldn't help but feel as though he were on a family trip, this being the family he wished he'd had. The one he could have had if he'd stepped up and told Andi how he'd felt about her so long ago. Or maybe this was how things were meant to be. Perhaps if he'd told her his feelings back when they were practically still kids, she'd have turned him down and they'd never have made their way to... *this*.

Whatever this was between them, it was the beginning of something good.

The day wound to a close, and of course Nicky

wanted to go sleep at a friend's, but because it was a school night, Andi vetoed that request, so they headed back to Andi's house. She invited him to stay for dinner, which was just going to be pizza, and he found himself hanging out with them both during the afternoon until after they'd eaten and she sent Nicky upstairs to shower.

She settled down beside him on the sofa in the family room and groaned. "Long day. But fun. Thank you," she said. "I appreciate you including Nicky in our day."

He studied her, her cheeks pink from the day outdoors, her eyes glittering. "My pleasure. He's part of you, so he's important to me, too."

Tears filled her eyes at that. "It's a rare man who can accept another man's child that way. Especially given our history."

"I look at him and I only see you."

She smiled, his answer obviously pleasing her. His next question wouldn't, but he decided to ask it anyway. "So Gary, the police officer…"

The smile faded from her face. "What about him?"

"He said he hadn't expected to run into you again this weekend. What did he mean?" Because Kyle had a hunch Gary hadn't been in to the shop to buy flowers. That wasn't *running into her* when she worked there.

"I took a self-defense class yesterday at the police

station."

But she didn't meet his gaze. "And what made you decide to take the class now?"

He knew how busy she was, between work and Nicky, and with Billy long gone, he assumed her life was simple and uncomplicated. Unease prickled along his spine.

She twisted her hands together and clearly forced herself to look into his eyes. "You're going to get upset."

He nodded, bracing himself. "Just tell me."

Blowing out a breath, she blinked hard. "Phoebe told me that Billy listed his mother's house with her company and he's back in town."

He realized he'd already expected her news to have something to do with her ex, and a mix of emotions rushed through him. Anger that they had to deal with the bastard again. Frustration that the son of a bitch was back at a time when Kyle was just getting past Andi's fears and walls, and hurt that she had obviously hidden the news from him... just as she'd never told him why she pushed him out of her life in the first place.

He drew a deep breath, taking a minute to gather his thoughts, because the last thing he wanted to do was scare Andi in any way.

He couldn't control the clench of his jaw, though,

as he met her gaze. "Why didn't you tell me as soon as you found out?" He withheld the anger but couldn't prevent the hurt from coming out in his tone.

She swallowed hard. "He's my problem, Kyle. Not yours."

"Isn't thinking that what broke up our friendship to begin with?" He reached out and grasped her hand in his. "I'm not pressuring you into more than you can handle relationship wise, but we're rebuilding something different than just a friendship, and if you're going to hide things from me again, it destroys that fragile trust."

She blinked away tears and he caught one with his fingertip. "I just feel like I got myself into this – despite your warning – and I should be the one to get myself out of it."

He shook his head. "People make mistakes. That doesn't mean you shouldn't rely on friends and family when times get tough. And if we're going to have anything between us, there can't be lies this time. Or things unsaid."

She inhaled and nodded. "It's going to be hard to undo years of hiding. But I promise to try."

"That's all I can ask for." He exhaled hard, then asked, "Have you seen or heard from him?" Because he wouldn't put it past her to hide that from him, too.

She swallowed hard. "Maybe?"

He cocked an eyebrow and waited for an explanation.

"That night we were at the Blue Wall? I thought I saw him but I told myself I was imagining things. And it was before Phoebe had told me he was in town, so I had no reason to think he'd returned." She bit down on her lower lip and drew it into her mouth.

He forced himself not to think of it as a sexy move, not when they were discussing something so serious. "Next time, you say something, okay?"

She nodded. "I hate that this is still part of my life."

"You've moved on. Just remember that and you'll manage whatever comes next." He tried to imbue his confidence in her, and knowing how important it was for her to stand on her own, he deliberately didn't say *we'll manage whatever comes next*. Even though it nearly killed him not to be able to step in and fix things for her.

She smiled and he leaned over and kissed her, pulling her into his arms. The kiss immediately turned hot, his tongue gliding along and tangling with hers. But she seemed to be holding back from him and he silently cursed her ex for returning and potentially ruining all the progress he'd made.

AFTER KYLE LEFT and Nicky turned in for the night, Andi poured herself a glass of wine and sat down in the family room, kicked her feet up, and sighed. What had started as a special day had taken a wrong turn. Any time Billy's name came up, her day was usually ruined.

She felt frustrated over so many things, past and present. She'd worked so hard to get over the fact that she'd let herself be abused without standing up and doing something about it. And she didn't know how to get past the notion that because she'd made this mess, she had to fix it herself. Maybe it came down to losing her mother when she was on the verge of being an adult, and though her brother did his best, she'd really had to learn to rely on herself. Instead of stepping up for his family, her father had fallen more deeply into his gambling, and she'd gotten together with Billy a short time after. Looking back, maybe she'd been vulnerable and hadn't realized it at the time.

But here she was now, the self-sufficient woman she'd had to struggle to become, a single mom, and the woman Kyle desired. Yet she feared losing him because she didn't know how to open herself up, while she also worried about losing herself *in* Kyle like she had in Billy. And then there was the overall concern about Billy's return and what that meant to her physically as well as emotionally.

For the first time, Kyle was asking for something from her and she had to find a way to give him what he needed, to share and not be so damned self-sufficient. She was torn between the need to stand on her own and the woman who wished she didn't have a painful past and could just throw caution to the wind and enjoy her life.

She took another sip of wine, and on that frustratingly complicated note, she decided to turn in for bed.

ANDI WOKE UP the next morning, last night's thoughts weighing heavily on her mind. She went about her morning routine and getting Nicky up and ready for school. No sooner had she dropped him off than her phone rang.

"Hello?"

"Hey, sis." Kane's voice sounded over the speakerphone in her car.

"What can I do for you this bright, sunny morning?" She hoped being optimistic would alleviate the worry over the fact that her brother rarely called her on the way to work. Unless it had to do with–

"Dad's on a gambling bender," he said, not beating around the bush.

She let out a sigh. She knew her dad's benders well, having lived with him until recently... until he'd disappeared one night with money from her wallet. She'd known at that point she couldn't go on staying in the same house and being aware of everything he did and said. She and Nicky had moved out but he'd continued to work at Kane's garage, which meant her brother knew her father's comings and goings. And they were both all too familiar with his gambling highs... and the lows that inevitably followed.

"Dammit," she muttered. They'd never been able to get him into a gambling program that stuck.

"He hasn't shown up for work in two days. I stopped by the house and he's not there. I decided not to go checking with his friends or looking for games this time. You're right when you said we have to live our own lives and let him live his. Which doesn't mean it's easy to do."

She let out a slow breath, in total agreement with her sibling. "You're doing the right thing," she assured him. "That's the reason I moved out. I couldn't be his mother." But it hurt her nonetheless.

She pulled into the parking lot behind the floral shop and cut the engine. "Is there anything I can do?" she asked, worried about her brother and her dad. But there was only one of them she could realistically help right now.

"No. I just wanted you to know and to ask you to call me if you hear from him."

"You know I will. Is Halley okay?"

"Great," he said, the only time in the conversation his tone lifted. "Not too nauseous, which is good."

"Well, that's good. Say hello and I'll check in with you later," she promised him. "Bye."

"Bye," he said, disconnecting the call.

She gathered her purse and opened the door, stepping out of the car. Aware of her surroundings now, thanks to the class she'd taken, and relieved to see other people by their cars in the large lot, she walked straight to the alley leading to the store.

She opened for the day, the sense of unease she'd had since yesterday staying with her, but there was nothing she could do except live her life, whatever that might bring.

Chapter Seven

ALMOST A WEEK later, on a Saturday morning, Andi was outside watering the flowers she had in pots on the front steps of her house. The orange pumpkins she'd picked with Kyle and Nicky blended well with the yellow and red Mums on either side of the steps, complementing the yellow siding on her house.

She didn't recognize the old beat-up car that pulled into her driveaway, and clearly her survival instincts weren't all that great, because she was shocked to see Billy step out of the driver's side.

She immediately started for the house when he called her name. "Andi, wait."

She glanced around, noticing her neighbors were outside, the one to the right playing ball with his son, one across the street watering flowers, too. And her son was at a friend's house. She'd dropped him off an hour ago, which eased her mind, at least as far as her boy was concerned.

Feeling safe enough with eyes on her, she straightened her shoulders and waited until he came close enough not to yell in order to converse. "That's far enough. You can talk to me from there."

He didn't look good. For a man who'd been a jock in his teenage years and who had taken pride in his appearance, he'd let himself go. A pot belly pushed against the old, long-sleeve shirt he wore over a pair of baggy jeans. And his sandy-blond hair had receded more than she remembered, a greasy sheen covering the strands that remained. At just the sight of him, she wanted to wrap her arms around herself for protection, but she held on to the watering can, refusing to show him she was afraid.

"What do you want?" she asked in the wake of his silence, during which he'd obviously been taking in her appearance, as well.

"I came to see my wife."

"Ex-wife," she reminded him.

"Right. And I admit, when I came home to sell Mom's house, I didn't plan on seeing you."

"Then why didn't you stay away?" she asked.

"I would have until I saw you and Davenport together at the Blue Wall. You and I had an agreement and you went back on our deal."

She blinked at him, completely blank as to what he could mean. "I don't understand."

"I told you to stay the hell away from him and you agreed."

"Back when we were together!" she said, shocked he'd even care who she saw or what she did now. "We've been apart for two years. Last I heard, you were involved with another woman. Why do you care what I do or who I see anymore?"

He cracked his knuckles, a gesture she was too familiar with, and it was all she could do not to run for the safety of the house. But Billy was respecting the distance she'd insisted on and the neighbors were still outside, so she forced herself to remain calm.

"I'm free again. My girlfriend and I broke up, but don't worry. I have no interest in taking you back. You've had a kid, put on a few pounds, and lost your shine. But nobody touches what was once mine. Especially him. Something about that pretty boy always got under my skin. Because I wanted you and he had you first."

His insults didn't faze her but his possessiveness despite the fact that he no longer wanted her wasn't a good sign. If he was single and he'd lost the woman who was funding his lifestyle, he'd be miserable and he'd want to make her feel the same way. He was a bully, a man who lived to push someone else around, and in the past, she'd been easy for him to abuse. He obviously thought he could pick up where he'd left off.

"Kyle didn't have me first, as you so crudely put it.

We're good friends. And you no longer have any right to dictate who I see or what I do. As a matter of fact, you never did."

"Wrong. Because if you keep hanging around with Davenport, I'll be sure to remind you what happens when you don't do what I say."

She knew what his reminders meant. He'd hurt her. When she least expected him to show up, he'd ambush her and make sure she knew he was the boss.

His eyes gleamed with what she could only call determination and that caused her stomach to churn, nausea overtaking her. "I know how to get what I want out of you, Andrea."

She gripped the plastic watering can tighter. He did. He knew how to get under her skin and have her flesh crawling as she waited for him to replace the emotional torture with the physical. She had the same old reactions to his threats now. Her stomach was twisting in fear and sweat popped up on the back of her neck, panic overtaking her, as she worried he'd hurt her.

But she refused to succumb to her fear again. "And this time I have no problem going to the police and telling them you threatened me."

"Why would they believe you?" he asked.

When they were married, he would reinforce the fact that he was a football hero in this town and people would trust his word over hers. Thanks to her fear and his fists and looming, hulking figure, she'd trusted in what he told her.

She'd come a long way since then. Not that she wasn't afraid. She was. She just wouldn't cower anymore. "Why *wouldn't* they believe me? I'm more than happy to tell them and we can find out. Come near me again and I'll let them know them you're harassing me. I'll get a restraining order. Don't test me, Billy. I'm not the same woman you were married to."

She'd surprised him into silence.

This was the furthest she'd ever pushed or defied him, but she wasn't worried he'd hurt her right now. He wasn't worked up or in a frenzy, nor was there latent anger beneath the surface. He was merely here letting her know he was back and that he expected her to jump right back to obeying him.

"Stay away from Davenport and I'll stay away from you."

She waited until he strode to his car, got in, and drove away before her knees nearly buckled. She walked to the house, grabbed the handle, and let herself in, turning the lock behind her.

Andi did two things next. She looked up and called an alarm company and convinced them of the urgency to install a security system today, and she dialed Kyle and asked him to come over so they could talk.

KYLE WAS SURPRISED to get a call from Andi asking him to come by. She sounded shaken up and he immediately headed over to her house. Everything looked quiet as he pulled his car up and parked in her driveway.

She answered and let him inside, looking around outside before closing the door behind them. She was pale, her hair looking as if she'd been running her fingers through it in agitation.

"What's going on?" he asked.

"Come on into the kitchen." She led him into the cheery room with sunshine coming through the window over the sink and the sliding glass doors leading to the outdoors.

He waited until they'd settled next to each other in chairs at the table before asking again. "What's wrong?" He leaned in close, knowing she was upset and he wasn't going to like what he heard.

She ran a hand through her unruly waves. "I had an unwelcome visitor earlier today."

He curled his hands into fists and hid them below the table. "What did the bastard want?"

She met his gaze, eyes wide. "Apparently he saw us together at the Blue Wall. He wanted to remind me that I'd made a deal with him. That I promised not to see you again and he meant to make sure I held up my end of the bargain."

Kyle clenched his jaw. "Are you fucking kidding me? He doesn't show his face for two years, agrees to a divorce, gives up custody of his kid, and thinks he can come back and tell you what to do?"

"Billy isn't happy. He lost the woman he left town with, and seeing us together, seeing me happy, well, that pissed him off. According to him, I was his and no one touches what was once his. Especially not you. Or something like that." She shook her head. "Look, I realize this makes sense to no one but him... and me because I've lived with him." She braced her hands on the table and pushed herself to a standing position, then began pacing around her small kitchen. "But I'm not giving into him again."

He drew a deep breath, processing what she'd told him, from her ex threatening her to the fact that she was going to stand up to Billy this time around. One made Kyle furious, the other proud.

"He threatened you?" He rose from his seat, anger flowing through him.

She stepped up close, putting a calming hand on his shoulder. "He just reminded me that if I don't do what he says, I know the consequences. That, yes, he'd hurt me." She sighed. "He let the memories do the actual threats for him." She shuddered as she spoke, telling Kyle how badly her ex had gotten to her.

"I'm going to pay that bastard a visit and make sure he understands he's not just dealing with you anymore. If he wants to touch you, he's going to have to go through me." There was no way he was going to let her walk around in fear anymore.

"No."

"What? Why not?" he asked.

She met his gaze, a stubborn tilt to her chin. "Because I've spent the last two years rebuilding my life and becoming self-sufficient and emotionally strong. If I let you fight this battle for me, I lose all the progress I've made. Billy needs to know that even if I'm afraid, I can stand up to him."

"How? He's bigger, he's stronger—"

"I took a self-defense class, remember?" She held up a hand. "And before you say anything, I understand it's not enough for me to really go up against a man Billy's size. But it gave me tools I didn't have before to look out for myself. And I have a security company coming by later to install an alarm system."

He had to admit he liked what he was hearing. She wasn't just posturing. She'd thought through how to protect herself.

"If he touches me or harasses me again, I promise I'll go to the police."

He blew out a deep breath, her words penetrating the haze of anger surging through him at her ex. He heard her, knew how important her independence was to her after what she'd lived through. And though Kyle hated taking a step back and watching this play out, he understood that if he didn't, if he kept pushing to take over, he would lose the progress *they'd* made.

He'd lose her.

"Okay," he said at last.

"Okay?" Obviously surprised, she met his gaze.

He clasped both her hands in his and looked into those big brown eyes. "I don't like it, but I understand why you need to handle it yourself. I respect your need to be strong."

"But?" she wisely asked.

He hoped she knew there was more to his feelings because they were getting to know each other again. To understand one another on a deeper level.

"But please don't ask me to turn my back and pretend none of this is happening. If you want me to respect your feelings about handling Billy, I need you to respect mine. And that means I'm going to be around a lot more often."

She frowned at the prospect. "To keep an eye on me."

He shook his head. "Actually, no. To keep an eye out for him."

She blew out a long breath and eyed him warily. "But you'll stay out of it?"

"Unless I see him bothering you, then all bets are off." He ran a hand over her wavy hair. "Agreed?"

She relaxed her shoulders and sighed, her defenses finally down. "Agreed."

He placed his hands on her hips and pulled her close. "Is everything else okay?"

She pursed her lips and sighed. "Well, my father is gambling again. That's never a good thing. He disappeared for a few days, turned up again on a high, according to Kane. Which means he'll keep going, thinking he's invincible."

"C'mere." He wrapped her in his arms, inhaling her alluring scent. "Are we alone?" he asked because he hadn't seen or heard Nicky since he'd arrived.

She nodded. "Nicky's at a friend's. He wasn't home when Billy came by, thank goodness."

He kissed her forehead. "We're going to get through everything together." He said it despite her insistence on dealing with her ex alone.

He said it because they were a couple, and even if she wasn't taking the relationship as one with a possible future, he was. And his goal was to get her to want the same thing.

The only way that would happen was if she understood he viewed her as the independent woman she wanted to be. Kyle just wanted her safe. To that end, if Billy laid a hand on her, there'd be hell to pay. But

Kyle was going to spend his free time showing her how much he valued her, by respecting the boundaries she set up. While still keeping an eye out for the son of a bitch who'd threatened her.

A TYPICAL BOYFRIEND brought flowers or chocolates to his girlfriend when he wanted to give her a gift. Kyle stopped by the flower shop on Monday and gave Andi a can of mace, and she couldn't be happier. To her, this was proof he understood her need to take care of her ex herself. Because if Kyle had continued to push to handle things, she would have been hurt and angry. Now she knew he trusted her to deal with her own life. That meant a lot to her.

Now her plan was to ignore the threat of her ex-husband and go on with her life. Nicky had gotten one hundred percent on a difficult reading test yesterday, and today she was picking him up to surprise him with a trip for ice cream after school to celebrate. Even though the weather had turned cooler, in her mind, it was always time for ice cream.

On a normal pickup day, parents waited outside of the school in a big group. Teachers brought the kids up to the exit, but it was impossible to see who each child left with. That was just how it had always been at the school, but she'd usually managed to grab her son as he walked out and there had never been a problem finding him.

She saw his smiling face as he headed for the exit and waved her hand so he'd see her. "Hey, Mom!"

"Hey, you. Good day?" she asked.

"Eh. Too much math homework."

She grinned. "Well, I'm going to make it a better one. We're going for ice cream to celebrate your reading test."

"Really? Cool!"

Before she could walk him through the crowd, she heard his name being called and they both turned to see Kyle making his way toward them.

"You left your math book on top of your desk," he said, handing the covered hardcover to Nicky.

"Oh." He blushed at the mistake and, at Andi's nudge, said, "Thank you, Mr. D."

"Thanks," Andi said, knowing Kyle could have left the book on the desk as a lesson for Nicky, to learn to remember his things and be more organized.

"We're going for ice cream," Nicky said.

Kyle's eyes opened wide with interest. "My favorite," he said. "And I'm hungry." He met her gaze, a deliberately pathetic smile on his face. "I could really go for some chocolate chip ice cream."

She rolled her eyes at his playful game. "Would you like to join us?" she asked.

"Oh, that'd be awesome," Nicky said.

"Let me think. I have work to do but..." Kyle deliberately paused. "Okay, you talked me into it," he said, laughing.

She shook her head, but of course she was glad to see him and would like for him to come with them.

"I'll meet you there," he said, winking at her before turning around and walking away.

She put her hand on Nicky's back and headed for the car, looking forward to their ice cream trip even more than she had been before.

They waited for Kyle at the store before ordering, Nicky choosing Rocky Road and Kyle choosing chocolate chip.

"Some things never change," she mused as she ordered mint chocolate chip for herself.

"What can I say? I'm a creature of habit." He shrugged and accepted his cone from the girl behind the counter.

Nicky had already gotten his and was sitting at a table playing with an iPad preinstalled at the counter, which Andi thought was a great idea for parents who brought kids into the store. Sometimes a mom needed a little downtime, and though she wasn't feeling that way today, she didn't mind that Nicky was enjoying himself on the gadget.

She'd gotten her ice cream in a cup and settled

across from Kyle at a small table near where Nicky played.

"Any special reason for the trip here today?" Kyle asked, licking at the vanilla that dripped down the cone.

"Just a special treat for Nicky's reading test grade," she explained. "I can't always spend after school with him if I don't have coverage at the shop. I did today, so it worked out."

He nodded in understanding.

She slid a spoonful of ice cream between her lips, his gaze on her mouth as she licked the minty cold treat off the spoon. She turned the plastic utensil and made sure to remove all the sweetness from both sides. A low growl escaped his throat and she froze at the sound, which was accompanied by a look of purely sexual heat in his eyes.

She didn't have to wonder what he was imagining. Her mouth on his cock. An intimacy they hadn't yet shared but one she had to admit she was eager to experience. And also one she shouldn't be imagining in a public place with her son nearby.

She cleared her throat. "Don't look at me like that," she said softly.

He leaned in close and whispered, "Like I want to eat you the way you're eating that ice cream? Or that I want you to—"

"Nicky, how's your cone?" she called out to him, despite knowing that her cheeks were probably a bright red.

"Good," he said over a mouthful of food, without looking away from the screen.

"He's not going to save you," Kyle said, laughing.

She shot him a wry look.

Before either could comment, the store door opened and Phoebe walked in. "I was walking by and I thought that was you," she said to Andi, walking up to the table. "Mind if I join you?"

"Of course not." Kyle rose and pulled out her chair for her and she sat with them.

"I have some news about the house we were discussing. I was planning on calling you anyway." Phoebe glanced over at Nicky and Andi got the message.

"Billy's mother's house," Andi whispered to Kyle. "Phoebe's office has the listing." She looked to her friend. "What about it?"

"We got an all-cash offer. A couple is moving to town and wants to get their child settled into school as quickly as possible, so they want the house. They don't even care that it needs work. They're more than happy to do it and Billy was willing to sell for cash. Title search, home and termite inspection, and survey all handled. It should close before Thanksgiving."

"Oh wow." Andi was startled. "That's fast."

Phoebe nodded. "It happens sometimes. Not often, but…" She shrugged.

"Maybe Billy will leave town once it closes," Andi murmured.

Kyle reached over and covered her hand with his. "We can hope."

She glanced over at Nicky, who was still involved in his game.

"Okay, I've got to head over to Jamie's soccer game," she said. "Glad I ran into you."

"Me, too," Andi said.

"Take care," Kyle said, rising as she stood. He sat back down again and glanced at Andi. "I was thinking."

"About?" she asked warily.

"Having Braden Clark look into Billy. See what he's up to now." Braden was Juliette's boyfriend and he owned a private investigation agency.

She shook her head. "I don't want to give Billy a reason to come after me. I don't want to show interest. Just have patience. Let this play out. If the house sells, he has no reason to stay here," she said, knowing she was relying on pure hope. But hope was all she had at this point.

He groaned. "You're killing me, tying my hands left and right," he said, his frustration showing through.

"I appreciate that you're respecting my wishes, though."

"Yeah," he muttered. "But if this escalates, we re-negotiate."

He squeezed her hand tighter and she nodded.

"Now when can I see you again?" he asked, moving his chair closer.

He didn't have to elaborate for her to know he didn't mean a family-type gathering.

"I told Nicky he could have a friend sleep over on Friday night, but the parents invited Nicky to come with them to the movies and sleep there instead. Which leaves me home alone," she murmured huskily.

He leaned in closer. "You've got yourself a date."

"Mom, I'm finished!" Nicky stood up from his chair at the same time Andi slid her chair back and away from Kyle.

It was one thing to go out together with her son, another to show any kind of public display of affection. It wasn't something she was ready to expose Nicky to. He'd ask too many questions about her relationship with his teacher, questions she wasn't ready to answer.

Not even to herself.

ANDI WAITED FOR Kyle to arrive on Friday, excited to be alone with him. This was time she was giving herself apart from being a mom, time with a man she desired and cared deeply for. That's all she would let herself think, for now. He wasn't pressuring her for a deep commitment, which meant she didn't have to think about what she was ready for in her life.

She showered and dried her hair, fluffing the waves she'd grown used to over the course of her life. She used her favorite moisturizer, getting ready for the evening. A light touch of makeup along with a casual outfit, jeans and a black tee shirt she didn't expect to keep on for long.

They weren't having dinner. She'd had to help set up the flowers for a party and came home late. He was just coming over to be with her.

The doorbell rang and she checked out the window before deactivating the new alarm and letting him inside. It was an adjustment to keep herself behind an alarmed door but well worth her peace of mind.

"Hi," she said, taking in his more casual look than what he wore for teaching – a pair of tight-fitting jeans and a pullover long-sleeve burgundy shirt. He was sexy in anything and tonight was no exception.

"Hi, yourself." He leaned in and pressed a hot kiss on her lips, one that wasn't just a peck hello but let her know how glad he was to see her.

Equally happy to see him, she laced her fingers around his neck and deepened the kiss, their mouths fused together, tongues mating. Her body quickened, desire filling her, liquid and thick in her veins. She threaded her fingers through his hair, her fingers tangling in the silken strands, keeping their mouths together.

She hooked a foot around his and pulled him closer, his groin nestling in the vee of her legs. She moaned at the delicious feeling of his body, thick and hard, telling her how much he desired her.

He picked her up and lifted her into his arms.

"No small talk?" she asked, teasing him.

His eyes gleamed with desire. "Not when I can finally see you naked again."

"I really can't argue with that," she said in a husky voice. She deliberately rubbed her breasts against his chest, her nipples stiff behind her bra, the sensation hot, shooting sparks of awareness throughout her being, dampness coating her panties.

He nipped at her bottom lip, then carried her into her bedroom. Her gaze never left his, his eyes hazy with yearning as he lowered her onto the mattress. He reached for the hem of his shirt and stripped it off. Taking a cue from him, she divested herself of her own clothes until she was naked.

He'd just finished doing the same and stood by the

edge of the bed, condoms he'd grabbed from his jeans in one hand. He tossed them onto the dresser.

"Do you know what I was thinking about the whole time I was licking at my ice cream the other day?" she asked, her gaze on his impressive erection, hard and straining upward, waiting for her touch. Or her taste.

"What?" he asked, voice hoarse.

"This." She crawled the few paces to where he stood, dipped her head forward, and licked at his cock like it was an ice cream cone.

His hand came to the top of her head as he groaned loudly. "Jesus, Andi. That feels so fucking good. Do it again."

"Who knew you had such a dirty mouth, Mr. Davenport?"

He chuckled and she stopped his laugh by pulling him into her mouth and swirling her tongue around his length. He slid his hand behind her head and began guiding her as he thrust his cock in and out of her mouth.

She closed her eyes, breathed in his masculine scent, automatically relaxing her throat as they found their rhythm. She'd hated doing this with Billy, had never even had the desire. And over time he liked to tell her how bad she was at it. But right now, this was Kyle and she wanted to give him this, was surprised by how much. And she didn't want to think about her ex now, just Kyle. And he wasn't complaining; instead he was lost in *them*.

He rocked his hips and she accepted as much of him as she could take, swallowing around the head of his cock. Gathering her hair in his hand, he pumped his hips faster and she swayed each time he thrust forward. Suddenly he pulled at her hair and she understood his warning, but she wanted to experience everything with him.

She stayed in place as he seemed to grow impossibly bigger and finally he let go, coming hard, and she swallowed as fast and as much as she could. He stilled and she glanced up at him, his eyes heavy-lidded with desire but also soft with an emotion she couldn't name.

She looked away, afraid of the intimacy between them and what it could mean, instead crawling back to the head of the bed and collapsing against the pillows. He joined her, pulling her into his arms, and she lay her head on his chest and sighed.

"That was incredible," he told her.

She felt a small rush of pride that she'd pleased him. She'd never had a good man in her life or her bed. Billy had taken her virginity, and Nicky aside, he'd left her with a bad feeling about men in general. But she instinctually knew Kyle was one of the decent ones. The kind who cuddled after sex and appreciated what went on between a man and a woman. Who did more than take what he could get, then roll over and snore afterward.

She sighed into his broad chest and he rubbed a hand over her back, his palm coming to rest on her ass. "I feel a second wind coming on."

She lifted her head and grinned. "Oh yeah?"

Another thing she appreciated about Kyle, his seemingly perpetual good mood. She didn't have to try and read his mind or figure out what kind of temperament he had on any given day. If he was upset about something, he told her. If he wanted something, he asked for it. And if he desired to give something, he just did it, not expecting anything in return.

"I can give you more time to rest," she offered cheekily. "You know, if you're tired."

Before she knew it, he'd flipped her onto her back and came over her, his eyes gleaming at what he'd probably deemed a challenge. "Not tired," he assured her. "Not with this gorgeous body waiting for me." He slid a hand around her breast, playing with the heavy flesh, tweaking her nipple between his fingertips.

She groaned.

"I like that sound. Does it mean what I think it does?" He slid a hand down her chest, over her stomach and through her damp sex. "Yep. Nice and wet for me," he said in a gruff voice. "Is that what going down on me did to you?"

She knew her face was all sorts of shades of red. "It turned me on," she admitted.

He reached over and grabbed the condom from the nightstand, opening it up and rolling it on before coming over her, his gaze hot on hers. "Then let's take care of you," he said, easing his cock between her thighs, where she throbbed with need.

She parted her legs wider and he pushed into her, gliding in easily because she was already so hot for him. "Does this feel good, pretty girl?" he asked, thrusting in deep.

"So good." She arched her back and moaned as he hit the right spot inside her that had her seeing stars. Bright, sparkly stars and she soared to greet them.

"Then let's give you more." He began to pump his hips, taking her higher with each grind of his body against hers.

This, too, was new to her, coming while having sex, feeling such incredible emotions overtaking her as she looked into the face of the man above her. It made the sensations she was feeling that much more sincere and amazing. Her body responded to everything about him as he thrust over and over, bringing her closer and closer to climax.

The vibrations inside her body were so intense she

curled her fingers into his skin, rocking her body against his each time they came together. It happened fast, almost without warning as a wave of sensation overwhelmed her and exploded inside her.

"Kyle, God, harder, harder," she said as he complied, thrusting deep, increasing the intensity of the waves and emotions swamping her, taking her places she'd never experienced before. He seemed to pick up his pace and suddenly he stiffened, coming as another surge took her over once more.

They were quiet in each other's arms afterwards, Andi aware of her still-pounding heart. He ran his fingers up and down her arm, his own breathing evening out slowly.

"Wow," she finally said when she thought she could speak again.

"Yep, wow." He hugged her tighter to him. "And before you ask, I can't say I'm up for another round just yet," he said, laughter in his voice.

She couldn't help but chuckle, too. "This was… unique for me," she surprised herself by speaking out loud, all the thoughts that had been running through her head during the act still there now.

"Unique how?"

She was glad she was facing his chest so she didn't have to meet his gaze during the admission she couldn't seem to hold inside. "Sex was never good for me before. I… Billy was my first."

He stilled. "Shit, Andi. I had no idea."

"You weren't supposed to." For as close as they'd been as teens, sex wasn't something they'd discussed. It had been a line they didn't cross. It was time they went there now. "I think that's part of the reason I stayed with him. You give someone that part of you… I don't know. I was stupid. We know that."

"No." His fingertips tightened on her waist. "You weren't stupid. He snowed you. That's what men like Billy do. In addition to going after people weaker than them. I know he threatened me back then, but the truth is, he'd never have tried to hurt me. He just used your fear against you."

She nodded. "That he did." She drew a deep breath. "But sex was just that. It was sex. It was a shitty first time, which he blamed on me, of course, because I was a virgin, to shitty all the time, which remained my fault. Because I didn't know what I was doing. Because I was frigid."

"Andi–"

"No. I want to tell you all this before I lose my nerve." She was surprised at herself, at how much she wanted to unload the past she'd kept hidden.

When her first time with Kyle had been so incredible, she'd managed not to think of Billy or the criticism he'd always heaped on her during sex. She'd pushed herself to be brave and enjoy. She'd just wanted to revel in her time with Kyle, not dwell on the past. But now, with new and unexpected emotions swamping her, she couldn't help but need to go there and maybe put those demons to rest.

"Okay," he said, his tone telling her he understood and wanted to hear… but he knew he wouldn't like it.

"What we just shared, that was new and enlightening."

"Come here." He pulled her up so they were face-to-face and she was forced to look into his eyes. "It was enlightening not only because it was good sex."

"I know," she whispered, understanding that there had been emotions involved between her and Kyle, deep, serious emotions.

And that she should be running away from them far and fast. Because she'd already had one man who had control over her by instilling fear… and now she was afraid Kyle could take over her life just because it would be so easy to let him.

She pushed herself to a sitting position, wondering what to do next in light of all those realizations.

"I'm hungry after all that exercise," Kyle said. "Does Chinese sound good?"

And just like that, she found herself calling for delivery and killing time before the food arrived in very inventive ways, thoughts of putting distance between them pushed aside. For now.

Chapter Eight

ANDI WALKED INTO the new restaurant that had opened near the waterfront to meet up with Halley, Phoebe, and Juliette. The goal was to have a girls' lunch and to discuss Thanksgiving plans. They were all family, after all. Andi being Kane's sister and Halley's sister-in-law made her indirectly related to Halley's sisters, Phoebe and Juliette. Although Andi considered all three women friends, as well. Thanks to Billy, she hadn't had many of those in her life, so she didn't take these women or their presence in her life for granted.

They looked like they had just gotten seated, Halley adjusting her handbag on her chair and Juliette just lowering herself into her seat.

"Hi," Andi said, joining them, settling into the empty seat at the round table.

"Hi," each of the women said.

"I need a glass of water. I'm so thirsty." Juliette glanced around the restaurant, looking for a waitress. Catching sight of someone, she raised a hand in the air and the woman came over, taking their drink orders, too.

Nobody ordered alcohol, Halley because she was pregnant, the rest because they all had to work this afternoon, choosing a variety of other drinks. Halley and Andi ordered seltzer, Phoebe a cranberry juice, and Juliette a diet cola.

"So, how is everyone?" Phoebe asked.

Busy seemed to be the consensus. They talked about their jobs and their husbands, boyfriends, and kids and ordered lunch.

"I'll have the chopped salad," Juliette said.

"Oh, me, too," Phoebe said, closing her menu.

"I'll have a Greek salad," Andi said.

The waitress wrote down the orders. "Anchovies on that?" she asked.

Andi nodded. "Sure."

"Umm, would you mind passing on those?" Phoebe asked.

Andi shot her a questioning look. "Why?"

"Because the thought of them makes me nauseous," she muttered.

Andi shrugged and looked up at the woman taking their orders. "No anchovies."

"And for you?" she asked Halley.

Halley stared at the menu for another few seconds. "Grilled chicken, lettuce and tomato." She handed the plastic listing over to the waitress. "And French fries, please."

The other woman wrote down the order and smiled. "Thanks. Let me know if you need anything."

She walked away, leaving them alone.

"So, let's talk Thanksgiving," Phoebe said. "I'd love to have it at my house." Her husband, Jake, a general contractor, had purchased a house that was in a gorgeous wooded area that Phoebe and her son, Jamie, had moved into after they got married last Christmas.

"I–" Andi had been about to say she would have offered her home, small as it was, but whatever they all wanted worked for her, too, when Halley spoke.

"Kane and I really want to host this year," she said, glancing at her older sister. "Think I can steal it away from you?"

Juliette looked between them. "I'm in Aunt Joy's guesthouse, so I'm going to leave the arguing to you two."

Braden's dad had been deteriorating with Alzheimer's and he'd moved into a facility that could handle his situation. Since Braden had been living with his dad to help him, he'd wanted to start over in his own place. But Juliette, like Andi, knew better than to get between the two bickering sisters over the location of their holiday dinner.

Phoebe frowned. "But I was really looking forward

to a dinner as a family in my house."

"As was I. You can have next year," Halley said, trying to placate her sister.

"But I'm pregnant… and it would mean a lot to me to have my family around me at my place," Phoebe said, tucking a strand of her white blonde hair behind her ear.

The table was stunned into silence, Halley the first to speak. "And you're not just saying that to convince me to give up first dibs?" she asked obviously only half kidding.

Andi grinned, already getting excited at the unexpected news. But she couldn't help but marvel at the way these two spoke to each other. One would think they'd grown up together, doing all the sibling arguing and experiencing the rivalry of typical families. Instead they'd been separated as toddlers, sent to foster care, Juliette being taken home by her real father and lied to. She hadn't known she had sisters until this past summer.

Phoebe's mouth opened wide. "Are you joking? Of course I'm telling you the truth! I'm pregnant!"

Halley squealed out loud, the news sinking in. "We're going to have babies at almost the same time!" Disagreement forgotten, she jumped up and went to hug her sister, but Juliette had gotten there first. What ensued was a genuine crying-hugging-fest that included

Andi.

"I'm so happy for you and Jake!" she said, getting her chance to squeeze Phoebe tight.

Eventually they all sat back down, realizing they had made a scene in the middle of the restaurant.

"The lengths some people will go to in order to get their way. Upstaging my own pregnancy," Halley said, laughing, as their meals arrived, a genuinely happy smile on her face. "Thanksgiving at your house this year," she said to Phoebe.

"We can all bring a dish or two, make things easier on you," Andi said.

Everyone agreed, throwing out ideas for what their specialties were in the kitchen.

"Is everyone going to the tree lighting in town this year?" Juliette asked. "It's my first one and I'd love to go knowing you're all going to be there."

"We're taking Jamie," Phoebe said of her and Jake.

Halley glanced at her sisters. "It isn't something I used to do." She'd been very much of a loner before getting together with Kane. "But I'd love to go this year. I'm sure I can convince Kane to come. Andi? What about you?"

"Nicky and I always go," she said. Or they had since Billy had left town. She planned to attend this year and hoped he made himself scarce.

"Great!" Satisfied, Juliette picked up her fork and

they turned their attention to the food on their plates.

They ate, Andi forcing the salad down over the happy lump in her throat. She was so thrilled for Phoebe and the fact that she would be part of this baby's life as well as Halley and Kane's. Something that wouldn't have been possible had she still been married to Billy. If she hadn't retaken control of her life and gotten close to her family once again.

She hadn't heard from Billy again since that day at her house and she assumed it was because she hadn't been out in public with Kyle, therefore she hadn't given him a reason to push her further.

She wondered what Kyle was doing for Thanksgiving. It wasn't that she *needed* him in her life, but she did like having him there. But she knew he had his family to spend the holiday with and she told herself that was a good thing, that she wouldn't miss spending the day with him.

His smile.

His good humor.

His sex appeal. And he had plenty of that.

She sighed out loud.

"Andi, what's wrong?" Halley asked. "That was a deep sigh."

She glanced up. Realizing she'd been caught daydreaming about Kyle, she blushed, what she was sure was a deep red.

"You're flushed. What are you thinking about, Andi?" Juliette asked.

"I bet it's about Kyle," Phoebe said, sounding certain, and Andi didn't see the point in denying it.

"Can we change the subject?" she asked instead, enjoying the time she had with the women she called friends.

ANDI SUNK DEEP into the bathtub, letting the heat surround her body and sighed. Today had been a long day, with a lot of preparing of orders and being on her feet. It had been exhausting. She closed her eyes and enjoyed the relaxation, knowing Nicky was in his room reading and she had this time to herself.

Her cell phone rang and she dried her hand and picked it up. Seeing it was Kyle, she answered. "Hello?"

"Hi, gorgeous. What did I catch you doing?"

At the sound of his voice, her body reacted, nipples puckering, her sex clenching with need. "I'm in the bath," she said.

"Don't tease me with that vision," he said, a low groan rumbling from deep in his chest.

"I can't help it. You asked me what I was doing and I'm bathing."

Another groan sounded over the phone. "Are you

slick and soapy?" he asked gruffly.

"Not yet." She glanced at the bottle of bath soap on the ledge.

"Don't you think you should be? Do me a favor and pour some of that delicious peach-smelling stuff on your hand and rub it over your body."

She rolled her eyes. "I can't exactly do that with the phone in my hand."

"Then put me on speaker... low..." he said, knowing she wasn't alone in the house. "And put the phone on the side of the tub."

She blinked, wondering for a brief moment if it was the smart thing to do, then she lowered the volume so only she could hear and placed it on the porcelain edge.

Then she picked up the bottle and squeezed a generous amount of body wash into her palm.

"What are you doing?" he asked.

She swallowed hard. "Soaping myself up," she said, as she ran her hand over her arms and chest.

"Where is your hand?"

She ran her tongue over her lips, her sex throbbing as she answered. "On my chest."

"Cover your breasts with soap," he said, and she did as he instructed, gliding her palm over her breasts, first one, then the other.

"Don't forget your nipples, Andi. Coat them with

soap and rub them between your fingers."

Cheeks flaming, phone sex brand new to her, she pinched her nipples, slicking her fingers over them and rubbing them back and forth until her hips were rocking in time to the movement. She squeezed the tight buds harder, her sex growing heavy with need, and she moaned, a low, needy sound she was surprised came from inside her.

"Jesus," he muttered.

She heard the sound of a zipper and realized he was undoing his pants and probably gripping his cock in his hand. Sweat broke out on her upper lip.

"Now pretend your hands are my hands and slide them down your stomach. Slowly."

She inched her fingers down, over her rib cage, her stomach, past her belly button, until her fingertips approached her sex. Her clit pulsed in anticipation, and as she brushed her finger over the hardened tip, she sucked in a rough breath.

"That's me," he told her. "Those are my fingers sliding over your wet clit. Rub in circles," he said, his voice rough with desire.

"Kyle," she moaned, her fingertip doing as he told her, brushing over and around the hardened tip, desire overwhelming her more than when she'd pleasured herself before. When she'd been alone.

"Andi, fuck," he gritted out, and she knew for certain he was jerking off as he instructed her how to make herself come.

He continued to whisper sexy instructions in her ear but she barely heard. It was his gruff tone and the sensation caused by her fingers and the bucking of her hips that consumed her, along with the knowledge that he was building toward his own orgasm, too.

"Slide your finger inside you," he said, a bit louder, as if he knew he needed to reach past the desire soaring through her.

She pushed her finger into herself, curling it forward, her thumb on her clit, and she began to buck and rock, harsh breaths and moans escaping her throat.

"Now you're going to come for me," he told her.

She slid her fingers faster, harder, pumping her other finger into her, and came suddenly, the glorious waves of desire taking her up and over, her climax exploding throughout her body.

And all the while, Kyle's voice accompanied her, "That's it. Come hard. Pretend it's me fucking you."

She pinched her clit at the same time he groaned. "Aah, damn, Andi," he shouted, obviously coming, too.

By the time she collapsed into the cool water, spent and completely overtaken, it was as if Kyle had been there himself. As if it had been his fingers on her nipples, her belly, her clit… and inside her.

"Are you okay?" he asked roughly.

She leaned her head against the tub and sighed. "Totally relaxed," she murmured.

"Can't say I expected this when I called," he said with a low chuckle. "But it was damned good."

"Like I said, you talk dirty, Mr. Davenport. I have to get out of the tub. It's too cold now."

"Okay, I'm going to come by the store tomorrow. I want to ask you something and I'm too wiped out to deal with it now."

She smiled, knowing she'd given him the same explosive orgasm he'd provided for her. "Then I'll see you tomorrow."

✧   ✧   ✧

ON FRIDAY LUNCHTIME, Kyle's gaze darted around the street as he approached In Bloom, and the street was crowded, but he still looked out for Billy, not trusting the other man to leave Andi in peace. In fact, the longer things were quiet, the more nervous Kyle got.

He stepped into the shop and waited for Andi to finish helping two customers before she would have time to talk to him. In between, she fielded phone orders. He watched her work, her warm personality evident as she talked to the man and then the woman who were purchasing flowers. Her lively curls bounced as she pointed out various items in the refrigerated case behind her. She might not have had any experience when she'd taken this job, but she'd clearly learned her way around flowers and it was obvious why she was now the manager.

Finally, the store emptied out and he strode over to the counter and leaned an elbow on top. "Busy day?" he asked.

She laughed. "Not as much as it looked like when you came in. It's just the lunch-hour rush. Let's talk before it gets crazy again. What's up?" she asked.

"Well, I know it's still a few weeks away, but my mother is planning for Thanksgiving already and I wanted to invite you and Nicky to have dinner with my family. Just Mom, Dad, and my brother, Chase. And me." He looked at her, hoping she would say yes.

"Oh, Kyle. I wish I could but my family had the big holiday conversation, too. And with Kane married to Halley, it includes the other Ward sisters, too. It's a big family gathering. I even thought about asking you to join us but I know your mom would be devastated if you weren't with her on the holiday."

Disappointment filled him but he understood. "You're right about my mother," he said. "And I know you need to be with your family. What about dessert? Can I steal you and Nicky away?"

She paused in thought, then nodded. "Sure. That would be great. I'd love to spend time with you and your family, too."

He grinned and he knew it was a fucking huge one as he leaned closer to her. "Well, good. That's settled."

Before she could reply, the bells over the front entrance rang, announcing a customer.

To both their surprise, Billy walked into the shop and stopped halfway to the desk. "Well, look who doesn't take instruction well." His gaze darted from Kyle to Andi.

Kyle stiffened at the sight of the one-time athlete who'd obviously gone soft, as he rocked back on the heels of his feet, hands clenched in tight fists. He was ready to fight if that's what it took to keep the man away from Andi for good.

He glanced at her, noticing her eyes had opened wide.

"What are you doing here?" Kyle asked.

"It's a flower shop. I'm here to look at some flowers. And I can't help but notice that you two were looking cozy when I walked in."

"Notice whatever you want, Billy. Unless you're buying something, I'd like you to leave." Andi straightened her shoulders as she faced her ex.

"It's a store and I'm browsing."

She placed her hand on the phone on the counter.

"Buy something or leave. Otherwise I'm calling the police and telling them you're harassing me."

When he glared but didn't move a muscle, Kyle stepped into the man's personal space.

Andi gasped, clearly not wanting a confrontation, but someone had to make things clear to the man.

"You and Andi have nothing to discuss. You have no business with her, personal or otherwise. Now, if you'd like to buy something in this store, I can't stop you. But if you're just here to threaten or bully her with your presence, that I can do something about." He debated for half a second before grabbing the front of Billy's shirt and getting up in his face. Because Billy Gray had to know Kyle wasn't afraid of him. He couldn't scare him into running away. "Understand?"

Billy shook himself free of Kyle's grasp. "Looks to me like the only one doing any bullying here is you. Of a customer," Billy spat out. But he didn't make a move to come after Kyle. "That's fine. I'll leave. Because Andrea knows the consequences of defying me, don't you, Andrea?" He glanced at her, focusing his words on the one person he wasn't afraid to go head-to-head with.

"Go away, Billy. Sell your mother's house and leave town. It's best for everyone and there's nothing left for you here," she said, trying to sound bored with her ex, but Kyle heard the tremor in her voice.

"Frighten her, threaten her, touch her, and you'll deal with me and the local cops. The days of you hurting her are over."

Billy straightened his shirt, narrowed his gaze, and stormed out of the store.

Kyle waited until the other man had disappeared from sight before turning back and striding over to Andi. He pulled her into his arms and held on tight.

"You shouldn't have provoked him," she said but she hugged him back.

He breathed in her familiar scent and pulled her closer. "He provoked you by showing up here. I was just giving him a taste of his own medicine. A man like him isn't going to go after me. He focuses on those weaker and more vulnerable. I merely warned him of the consequences of his actions," Kyle said, running a hand over her back.

"And he warned me about the consequences of mine."

"It's time, Andi. You need to file a police report. Let them know he's harassing you."

She drew a deep, shuddering breath and nodded. "Okay."

That was easier than he'd thought. Apparently Billy's reappearance had really gotten to her. "What if I meet up with you after work and we head over there together. Can you get someone to pick up Nicky after school?"

She nodded. "He's going home with a friend anyway."

He reached out and stroked her cheek. "It'll be okay," he promised her.

She didn't answer and it ate away at him that he couldn't automatically make things better.

The trip to the police station went smoothly, except for the fact that Andi had no proof of prior abuse or Billy's current stalking. Still, the officer was sympathetic, taking her statement, and because they were a small town, he promised to have a car drive by her house and business periodically throughout the day and night.

It gave Kyle some peace of mind but not enough. If he had his way, he'd move in with Andi until her ex was out of town and gone for good, but he knew better than to suggest such a thing. She had a young, impressionable son and he couldn't just sleep in her bedroom, and if he parked himself on the couch, Nicky would question why his teacher was spending nights there. Added to which, Andi wouldn't want to scare Nicky by telling him Billy was back and issuing threats.

And if those reasons weren't enough, there were Andi's personal issues. If he asked to stay, she'd assume he was questioning her independence, and he didn't want to upset the stability they'd found in their relationship.

He did, however, plan to keep a much closer eye on her and Nicky.

ANDI AND NICKY went for Sunday night dinner at Kane and Halley's house. She'd had to turn down an invitation from Kyle to have dinner with him because her family hadn't had time to get together lately and she hadn't wanted to say no to Halley and Kane. Andi had offered to do the dinner at her house, but Halley was a homebody and Andi didn't mind going over to their place on the beach.

She wanted to help, so she cooked Nicky's favorite, her sweet potato pie, and picked up dessert and brought it over to her sister-in-law's house. Halley was making a brisket and vegetables in the kitchen when they arrived.

Kane greeted them at the door and ushered them inside. "Hey, Nicky! Want to go outside and kick around the soccer ball?" he asked, always good for taking her son for one sports activity or another.

"I do!"

"I'll meet you outside. I just want to talk to your mom for a minute."

Nicky nodded and ran out the front door.

"What is it?" Andi asked, looking at him with concern.

He glanced at her sheepishly. "I'm worried about this dad thing. I just hope I learned enough with Nicky to get this right," he muttered into her ear.

Neither one of them addressed the fact that for the first seven years of Nicky's life, before Billy left, Kane hadn't spent as much time with his nephew as he would have liked.

Pushing that thought aside, Andi grew serious. "You're going to be an awesome dad. The best. Just like you're the best brother and uncle there is." Tears formed in her eyes. Her brother deserved this happiness and so much more.

He broke the hug and grinned at her. "Thanks. Now one more thing. I heard through the family grapevine you're having trouble with Billy. I just found out this morning that he's back in town and harassing you, and I don't appreciate having to hear it secondhand. I also don't like the fact that my wife kept the secret from me because she was worried I'd go after him." He frowned, his frustration obvious.

Andi bit down on the inside of her cheek. "I'm sorry. I was worried about the same thing as Halley. I didn't want you to get into a fight with Billy, so I didn't say anything."

He reached out and took her hands. "You isolated

yourself from us once before. I couldn't handle it if you did that again. And I know there's a lot I didn't figure out about your marriage and how he treated you until it was too late… and that's on me. But Andi, you have to let your family help you."

"That's a theme I've been hearing lately," she murmured.

"From Kyle, I hope?"

She nodded.

"People love you. Let them be there for you. It doesn't make you weak. In fact, it makes you stronger."

Tears rose in her eyes. "I love you," she said, hugging him for the second time that day.

"I love you, too. Now how is he bothering you?"

She swallowed hard. "He showed up at the shop on Friday and Kyle was there. He warned Billy to stay away from me. And we went to the police station afterwards and I filed a report. They have a marked car driving by the house when they can." But she was still looking over her shoulder constantly.

"And if he bothers you again?" Kane asked, his hands curling into fists.

She grasped one and massaged until he released his grip. "It's going to be okay. Don't go all overprotective on me." She kissed his cheek. "Now go play ball with Nicky."

He seemed to relax, his shoulders easing down.

No sooner had he walked out than her father walked in. "Hi, Dad." She was glad he was joining them, not off somewhere with his gambling buddies. "How have you been?"

"Pretty good, Andi. Pretty good. I'm on a lucky streak." He grinned, looking pleased with himself.

"Dad—"

He shook his head. "Nope. No lectures. I won ten thousand dollars on a scratch-off ticket. Ten grand, can you believe that?"

And she knew what he'd do with the money if allowed to keep it. "How about you give it to me to put away for you?" she suggested.

"Hell no. I'm on a winning streak. I'm not letting you or your brother get in the way of me adding to my winnings."

She rolled her eyes, knowing better than to argue with him. "Dad, just be careful. Don't end up owing the wrong people."

"Don't worry about me. I'll be fine." He leaned in and kissed her forehead. "Now I'm going out to hang with the boys."

She watched him go, wishing yet again there was a way to stop his gambling and knowing that there wasn't anything she could do. With a sigh, she headed to the kitchen to help Halley prepare dinner.

Chapter Nine

A WEEK LATER, Thanksgiving came, a big family affair that Andi enjoyed even more this year. She could really appreciate the fact that she had these wonderful people in her life and that she could celebrate with them. With Billy lurking around, and she had seen him watching her from his car and on street corners, she was well aware of how different her life had once been.

The women congregated in the kitchen of Phoebe's house, and the men hung out in the den area, where football games played on Phoebe's large-screen television. Dinner was a boisterous affair, with the two younger boys, Nicky and Jamie, hanging out at one end of the table and the couples sitting next to one another talking, while Halley's aunt Joy and Andi's dad spent their time chatting while they ate.

After dinner, Andi helped clean up and then she excused herself and Nicky to go to Kyle's for dessert. His parents were happy to see her and even his brother, Chase, who could often be cool to her when she ran into him in town, was on his best behavior.

His mom fussed over Nicky and slipped him a second piece of pumpkin pie with ice cream and Andi didn't say a word, merely let him enjoy. Their day had been too good for mom rules and worries to get in the way.

Nicky and Andi left Kyle's mom's house, with Kyle departing at the same time and insisting on following them home. She didn't argue. He'd been doing that more often since the incident with Billy, and she understood his concern and couldn't deny she found comfort in knowing someone had her back. She couldn't bring herself to think he didn't trust her to take care of herself. Not in light of her ex-husband's threats.

Once they were in the house and Nicky had gone up to his room, she turned to face Kyle.

"How was your day?" he asked, his fingers tangling in her hair.

"Really good," she murmured. "Your mother's pies are still the best."

"She went overboard today. I think she wanted to impress you and give you a reason to come back."

Andi wrapped her arms around his neck. "Does she think you're not enough of a reason?"

He narrowed his gaze. "Of course not. She was just adding incentive."

Andi laughed. "She doesn't have anything to worry about."

"Mom, can we watch a movie?" Nicky asked, running down the stairs and joining them.

She easily stepped out of Kyle's grasp. "Sure. Why don't you two decide which one."

They sat in the family room and watched *The Secret Life of Pets*. Nicky had begun to take Kyle's presence in their lives as normal and she wondered if she ought to have a more serious conversation with him about her relationship with his teacher. This wasn't an easy decision and she mulled it over, distracted from the movie, trying to decide for herself just what this relationship was to her. She'd avoided thinking about it, blaming the fact that she had other, bigger issues in her life to worry about, but that was an excuse. She was afraid to examine her feelings too closely, frightened of what she'd find.

Kyle possessed so many qualities she not only admired but was drawn to on an emotional level. If what she felt for him was only sexual, it would be so easy. She'd scratch an itch. She wouldn't bring him around her son outside of school. She wouldn't spend part of a holiday with his family. And she especially wouldn't give in to requests like, *please call me when you get home from work so I know you're safely in the house with the alarm set.*

She glanced over to the other side of the couch to see Kyle laughing at the antics on the screen, talking to

Nicky about the gang leader bunny named Snowball. He had the ultimate amount of patience for her son and she found that as sexy as his bare chest, toned body, and handsome face.

She no longer thought of him as her childhood best friend, but instead as the man she was falling for. And falling hard. How that had happened when she'd promised herself she didn't need a man in her life, that she could and would stand on her own, was beyond her.

Nor did she know what to do about it. What did it say about her if she got over one bad relationship only to jump right into another one, albeit a good one, without really spending enough time making it on her own? And what was *enough time*, anyway? Did being a couple necessarily mean she was giving up her independence?

With those questions preoccupying her mind, she missed most of the movie, which she'd seen twice anyway. When the show finally ended, she sent Nicky up to shower and get ready for bed. She cleaned up the popcorn they'd made and Kyle helped her bring the soft drinks into the kitchen and put everything in the sink.

"They're lighting the town Christmas tree a week from Sunday," he said. "They picked a sixth grader to pull the switch this year and turn on all the lights."

She smiled. "Sounds like fun. I know Nicky wants to be there. He asked if he could go with his friend's family but I feel like I should take him myself."

Kyle propped himself against the kitchen cabinets and met her gaze. "Then let's do it. We can go together and he'll run into his friends when he's there. We'll make it a family day."

She bit down on her lip, her earlier conflicting thoughts still swirling in her head. Should she take her son herself? Did she need to push aside what she wanted, which was to be with Kyle, and do things on her own just because Billy had tried to control what she did and who she saw? Or was making her own decisions about spending time with Kyle enough?

Was it emotionally dangerous to act as if the three of them were, in fact, *a family*? Would Nicky be hurt if things ultimately ended with Kyle? She already knew she would be. But he'd given her no reason to think this relationship wasn't serious for him. He'd guided her ever so slowly from casual to intense without her even realizing it.

"You're overthinking things again," he said, capturing her face in his hands so she met his gaze.

An embarrassed smile lifted her lips. "Guilty," she murmured.

"It's an evening outside, watching a Christmas tree be lit up. It's not a lifetime commitment," he said, teasing, but she felt certain she heard hurt in his voice.

Because she'd hesitated. Because she couldn't just have a relationship without worrying about what it meant. What it said about her as a woman. As a person.

She sighed. "I'm sorry. Yes, let's go see the tree." She was well aware that this event would be them making a public statement. One Billy would no doubt see if he was still in town. And though according to Phoebe he had closed on his house, she knew he was still lurking around.

"Are you worried about Billy seeing us together?" he asked, reading her mind.

"Worried?" She shook her head. "No, because I won't be alone. I'll be surrounded by people and you'll be by my side. Aware of it? Always."

He slid his hand into hers. "We make our statement. We're together and he can't dictate that fact. And we go about living our lives," he said with determination.

As she nodded, he pulled her into his arms. "I'm glad you spent some of the holiday with me," he said, changing the subject.

"Me, too." Despite her qualms about everything, being with Kyle felt right.

Suddenly the sound of the shower running resonated through the pipes in the walls. Obviously taking advantage of the few minutes alone while Nicky showered, Kyle backed her against the counter, his hips holding her in place, and covered her lips with his, devouring her with his tongue.

She raised herself up on her toes and kissed him back, sliding her arms around his neck and losing herself in the masculine taste of him, desire immediately building inside her. It never took long for her body to ignite around him, but the longer they were together, the more her feelings were involved, too. In fact, she was all emotion now.

He made her feel safe at the same time he aroused her, and she pressed her body against him, trying to get as close as possible with their clothes on. He slid his hand into the waistband of her jeans, his palms cupping her ass just as the shower water stopped and Nicky yelled down, "Mom, I forgot towels!"

Laughing, she stepped away at the same time he removed his hands, grinning at her as he did. "At least we weren't caught," he said with a chuckle.

"True. And I have to go rescue the wet boy. Be right back."

She headed upstairs and retrieved freshly washed bath towels from the closet and handed them to Nicky. She returned downstairs to see her phone in Kyle's hand. "It was buzzing. It's your brother."

He handed her the device and she answered. "Hello?"

"Andi?"

"Kane? What's up?" she asked, suddenly alert. Because she'd been with her brother all afternoon. It wasn't like him to call after just spending the day with her.

"Dad got a phone call and left here in a mad rush, a huge grin on his face."

"A card game," she said on a sigh.

Kyle placed a comforting hand on her shoulder.

"That's my best guess. Want me to go hit all his usual places and bring him home?" her brother asked.

She shook her head. "You stay with your pregnant wife. It's been a long day."

"He's going to risk his scratch-off winnings," her brother said with frustration.

"And there is nothing we can do to stop him."

Kane muttered something she couldn't make out, probably a few choice curse words.

"How was the rest of your holiday?" she asked, changing the subject.

"Nice. Yours?" Kane asked, just as Kyle stepped up beside her and nuzzled her neck with his lips.

Her body reacted instantly, nipples puckering and an answering desire pulsing between her thighs. "G-o-o-d," she stammered, elbowing him playfully. "Stop it," she said when he licked the skin along her collarbone.

"Sounds like it's still going on," Kane said. "I'll let you go. Just give me a call if you hear from Dad and I'll do the same."

"Will do." It seemed like they had this same conversation often, but there really was nothing more they could do than commiserate and hope for the best.

She disconnected the call and met Kyle's understanding gaze. "I was just trying to lighten the mood," he said by way of explanation.

She chuckled, her body still alert and aware thanks to his seductive if not timely touch. And lick.

"Anything I can do to help?" he asked.

She shook her head. "Nothing's changed since we were kids. We just try and deal with his gambling better now."

He squeezed her hand in support and she tipped her head upward. "Are you sure you want to be involved with me? I come with an awful lot of baggage." Her ex-husband and his threats, her father and his vice, not to mention the fact that she was a single mother with all the responsibilities that entailed.

"Do you feel the connection between us?" he asked, his darkened eyes serious.

She nodded. With every fiber in her being.

"Then what makes you think I wouldn't be one hundred percent certain I want to be with you?" He pulled her close, his body heat comforting her. "You're worth everything that comes along with being in a relationship with you. In other words, you're not getting rid of me."

She wrapped her arms around his waist and laid her head on his chest. "And I don't want to."

She just couldn't shake the premonition that something bad was lurking just around the corner. Something like her ex. Or her father's excessive gambling that could send her spiraling in ways she didn't expect.

ANDI WAS FAST asleep when her doorbell rang. Panic raced through her as she pulled on a robe and tied it around her waist. Her cell phone in her hand and mouth dry, she walked to the front door and looked outside, prepared to see her ex-husband, relief filling her when she realized it was only her father.

She flipped on the hall light, deactivated the alarm, and opened the door, pulling him inside and locking it again behind them. "What are you doing here so late? It's almost midnight and you scared me to death!"

"Andi, I had the best luck!" His golden-brown eyes, so similar to her brother's, flashed with excitement.

"Shh! Nicky's sleeping," she said to him.

Her father nodded but it didn't dim his excitement. "I made a small fortune and I had to share the news with you."

Anger welled up inside her. "You woke me and you frightened me just to tell me you were gambling? I know that! And you know how I feel about it." She reached for the doorknob, intent on asking him to leave.

"You're going to feel differently when you find out who I won it off of," he said, pulling wads of cash from the inside lining of his jacket.

She blinked in shock. "Dad! You can't walk around with all that cash. It's just not safe!" And on that note, she set her burglar alarm.

"Don't you want to know who my patsy was?" His cheeks were flushed red with excitement.

She groaned. "Fine. Who was it?"

"Your bastard of an ex-husband," he said almost gleefully.

Andi pinched the bridge of her nose, feeling a headache starting. "Dad, you're telling me you saw him sitting at the table and you didn't walk away?"

He shook his head. "I told you I was on a roll. Who better to take for a ride? Son of a bitch had the money he'd gotten from selling his mother's house. He was trying to add to it. Rumor has it he's gotten himself in some trouble and needs to leave the country."

"Oh my God." So he was in town to sell the house, get as much money as he could put together, and leave, harassing her while he was here just because he could.

Well, that explained some things, she thought. But leave the country? "What kind of trouble?" she asked.

"I don't know and I don't care. But I do want you to have the money you should have had in the divorce. This can make life better for you and Nicky."

Her dad, who never parted with extra money if he was in a gambling phase, handed her more cash than she'd ever seen in her life.

She narrowed her gaze, her focus on her father and the wad of money in his pockets. Everyone he'd played at that table with knew he was walking around with big bills on him and it wasn't safe. To top it off, she knew taking anything from Billy was a double-edged sword. And he wouldn't let this loss go unpunished.

Hating to do it at this late hour, she turned her phone on and called her brother. "Kane? Dad's here. I'm going to need you to come over," she said over her father's blustering objections.

Kane showed up fifteen minutes later. Andi deactivated the alarm and let him inside, resetting it behind him. She gestured to the money her father had spread out on the table in the family room.

"Holy shit." He stared from the cash to his father.

"He won it off of Billy," Andi whispered.

That renewed her brother's cursing. "Dad, that bastard now has every reason to come after Andi. What the hell were you thinking?"

"It was a card game, Kane. I play them all the time. He lost fair and square."

But Billy had a temper, and if he needed the money for serious reasons, this was definitely going to be an issue, Andi thought, her stomach churning.

"Okay, for now I'm going to take this money and put it in the safe at the garage," Kane said. "And tomorrow we're going to figure out how to get the money back to Billy."

Their father started to open his mouth to argue, then wisely shut it again. Maybe he was starting to realize the magnitude of his mistake, playing cards against Andi's ex. He meant well, he always did, but he'd screwed up big this time.

THE FRIDAY AFTER Thanksgiving was a big local shopping day and Andi opened the store herself. Although she knew from experience most people bought their floral arrangements before Thanksgiving, it still made sense to be open just in case. Her plan was to work half a day. Nicky would be at his friend's in the morning and Wendy, the owner, wanted to take the afternoon shift. Apparently she had family over and needed a break from her company. After her own shift ended, Andi would pick the boys up and bring them back to her house so Nicky's friend's mom could do some Black Friday shopping herself.

She was sitting around in a quiet shop, no customers and no deliveries to make up, when the phone rang. "Hello?"

"Andi? It's Katrina." The mom who had Nicky over this morning.

"Hi, Katrina. Everything okay?"

"No," the woman said, her voice trembling. "The boys were outside playing in the backyard and Michael came running inside to tell me a man came and took Nicky."

The blood drained from Andi's head, and even sitting, she thought she might faint.

Katrina went on. "He said Nicky recognized him and didn't want to go, but the man grabbed his arm and pulled him toward the car. They were gone by the time Michael ran inside and told me. I'm sorry, Andi. I–"

"It's okay. You didn't do anything wrong. I know who it is," she said, somehow keeping her composure. "And I'll handle it." She disconnected the call. All she could think about was how terrified her little boy must be.

Before Andi could consider what to do next, her cell rang again with an unfamiliar number. Tingles ran up her spine as she answered, no doubt in her mind who was on the other end. "Give me my son, you bastard."

"Give me my money," Billy shot back.

That was a no-brainer. "Fine."

"Meet me in the park at the tree where we engraved our names."

The tree was in a secluded part of the park, nowhere near the gazebo where people met and congregated. Her heart pounded so hard she could hear it in her ears. But with fear for her baby lodged in her chest, she had no problem agreeing to his terms. "Fine but let me talk to Nicky."

"No."

"I'm not giving you anything unless I hear he's okay. From Nicky himself."

Billy cursed and she heard fumbling.

Then the best sound she'd ever heard. "Mommy?"

"It's me, baby. Are you okay?" she asked him, her hands shaking so hard she could barely hang on to the phone.

"I'm scared," he admitted.

"I'm coming for–"

"That's enough. You got what you wanted. Bring me every penny your old man stole from me if you want to see him again," Billy said, clearly confident she'd do as he asked. "I'll call you with a time."

"Don't lay a hand on him or I'll–"

He cut her off, ending the conversation by disconnecting them. She hit end and, on autopilot, made a few calls. To her boss, to tell her she was closing up shop for a family emergency. To Kane because he had Billy's money.

And to Kyle because she needed him.

She asked them both to meet her at home.

Petrified, she still managed to think. To realize she was doing the one thing she'd never done back when Billy had terrorized her before. She was relying on other people. Trusting them to have her back. Doing what she used to think was weak and realizing instead it was making her strong.

Before she could ask Kyle or Kane their opinion, as she drove home, she called the police. Because she refused to let Billy get away with kidnapping her son.

Chapter Ten

KYLE ARRIVED AT Andi's to find Kane running out of his car, a black bag in his hand, and a police car parked in front of him as he pulled in.

He'd gotten a call from Andi. "Meet me at my house. I need you."

That's all she'd had to say. He'd dropped the papers he'd been grading and headed over to her place. Now he knew something serious had happened and panic set in. He ran up the lawn, not bothering to walk around and up the driveway and front walk. The door was open and he stepped inside.

A uniformed officer talked on his phone and Andi practically flew across the room and into his arms. Kyle held her tight and looked over her shoulder to Kane, who was pale. "What's going on?"

"Billy took Nicky." He went on to explain how his father had won money from Andi's ex at a poker game. Big money that the man wanted back. "Fucking irony is, I was going to contact the bastard if I could find him. No one wanted that money on our hands. We just got it from Dad last night." He shook his head in frustration.

Kyle wanted to strangle her bastard ex himself, but he stayed calm for Andi's sake.

Because she'd reported a kidnapping, he realized now, the state troopers had gotten involved, taking the case from the local police.

The dark-haired officer listened to the call and hung up, glancing around the room, his gaze landing on Andi.

She stiffened but straightened her shoulders and Kyle pulled her in tighter, proud of her for holding it together. Glad she'd called him instead of opting to handle this alone.

"Whoever was on duty when you reported the harassment at your local precinct dropped the ball," the man said. "He should have run a check on your ex. He's wanted in New York City for assault."

Shit. Bile rose up in Kyle's throat.

"And he has my son." Instead of falling apart, Andi pulled free of him and said, "I need to take him the money. That's all he wants. The money."

"Hell no," Kane said, looking to the cop for support.

It took everything inside Kyle not to join Kane and tag-team Andi, insisting she not be the one to show up with the money for her son. But if he'd learned anything during their time together, he knew that if he didn't support her now, he'd lose her forever. It was going to kill him, but he was going to let her be the independent woman she'd struggled so hard to become.

The officer shook his head. "Ma'am, I think we need to be there when he shows up to collect the money."

"And I think she needs to be the one to hand him the cash. Get her son and you can take him in after," Kyle said, showing her all the support he could.

"What the hell?" Kane asked, glancing at Kyle.

He'd just have to explain himself to the other man when this was over.

Andi shot him a surprised but grateful look.

"Think about it," Andi said. "The police will set him off. He might hurt Nicky," she said, her voice trembling. "If it's me, it'll go like he expects. There is no way he thinks I'd call the police. I never did when we were married. He thinks I'm too afraid of him. I can drop the money, get Nicky, and then the police can take him before he suspects a thing."

The officer frowned. "Tell me about the meeting point."

"There are trees all around. You can hide without a problem. Get there now, before he calls me with a time. I know I can handle this," she said, imploring the man.

"Let me talk to my superiors," he said, picking up his phone again. "A detective should be here any minute and we'll need reinforcements anyway."

The officer left the room to make plans and Kane glared at Kyle.

"She needs to do this," he said to her brother. "She needs to face him one last time and to show him she's not afraid. She'll have police backup. I don't like it either, but I understand it."

Andi walked up behind him and wrapped her arms around his waist. "Thank you," she whispered.

"You're welcome," he said and he hoped like hell he was doing the right thing.

KYLE SAT IN the back of a police cruiser hidden from where Andi was meeting Billy. An officer sat in the driver's seat, waiting for the call that would let them know the situation had ended safely.

Kane sat by Kyle's side, glaring at him the entire time. He didn't blame the other man. Kyle had taken Andi's side and encouraged her to be involved in a dangerous situation. And as he waited anxiously for things to be over, he decided he must have had rocks in his head for pushing for her to take the money and confront her ex.

Billy had texted her earlier with the time to meet

him, nine p.m., well after dark. And during the time in between, they'd found out that the assault charge he was wanted for had been on the woman he'd been dating since leaving Rosewood Bay. She'd been found beaten and unconscious on her apartment floor.

Kyle blew out a nervous breath.

"If anything happens to her, I'll kill you," Kane muttered.

"Thanks. Way to make me feel better." He turned to face Andi's brother. "Do you really think this is what I wanted?" He gestured out into the dark night, the moon barely visible in the sky above the trees.

"I know." Kane shook his head and grumbled, "But my sister's a damned stubborn woman. First she has to handle an abusive marriage alone and in secret and now she has to take a stand against him in the most dangerous situation, surrounded by police with guns ready."

His stomach churned at the word *guns*. "But it's her son," Kyle reminded Kane. "She'd do anything to get him back and I have to support her." Because he loved her.

Sitting in the back of this vehicle, petrified for Nicky and Andi, he was well aware of the fact that the people he wanted to be his family were out there alone and in danger.

He wanted to be there and felt fucking frustrated

that he couldn't be. "I'd have made the drop myself if there was any way it would have resulted in Nicky's safe return. But we both know what Billy would have done if he'd seen me instead of Andi."

More grumbling from the man beside him that ended in another begrudging, "I know. I'm just scared to death for her."

"Join the club." His heart was out there with Andi, and until she returned, safe and sound, he wouldn't get it back.

"She's been through a lot in life," Kane said, glancing at Kyle. "If you don't treat her right, you'll answer to me."

He had no problem with her brother's posturing. He wanted nothing more than to treat Andi like gold for the rest of their lives.

THE AIR AROUND Andi was cold as she stepped out of her car, bag in hand, yet she was sweating beneath her jacket. Fear lodged in her chest, but she told herself that Billy had never had any interest in his son before. All Nicky was to him now was a means to an end. As long as she handed over the money, he wouldn't hurt him. He hadn't hurt him. She'd tried to convince herself of that fact since the phone call telling her that her baby had been taken. If she didn't force herself to believe he was safe, she wouldn't be able to breathe. She wouldn't have the strength to help him now.

She walked toward the tree she and Billy had carved their names on when she was young and naïve and thrilled the high school quarterback was in love with her, and forced herself to pull in calming breaths as she waited for him to show up.

She knew there were two policemen waiting on opposite sides of where she stood by the tree, waiting to close in on Billy once she had Nicky out of the way.

Suddenly the sound of a car engine broke the silence around her. Although it was hard to make out in the dark, she assumed it was Billy and waited until he climbed out of the vehicle and she could be sure.

"Andi?" he called out.

"Right here."

He started toward her and she spoke into the night. "Bring Nicky or I'm not giving you the money." She tried to hang on to her composure and not sound as panicked as she felt.

"Do you really think you're calling the shots?" he asked.

"I have a gun." She blurted out the lie, wanting only to see her child. "Now bring Nicky with you and you can have your money. I don't want it and never did."

Despite the darkness, she held out the bag she and

Kane had stuffed the cash into for him to see. She kept the other hand in her jacket pocket. Her pretend weapon.

"Fine. Though I don't think you have the balls to actually use it." He flung open the back car door. "Come out here, you pain in the ass."

Her heart eased when she saw her baby boy, but nausea filled her as Billy grabbed his arm — a move Andi knew would leave bruises — and pulled him toward her and his bag of money.

Her brave boy didn't say a word. He just looked at her with wide, fearful eyes. She hated Billy for this. If she hadn't hated him before, she was filled with vitriol for what he'd done to her son.

"You've always been a pain in the ass and your father is no different. He cheated me out of my money. Hand it over."

She swallowed hard and held out the bag. "Let Nicky go."

Billy shoved Nicky hard in the back, sending his frail frame flying toward Andi. She released the bag, letting it drop to the ground, and grabbed her baby boy in her arms. She dropped to her knees, pulling him down with her, sobbing at the feel of him, safe and sound.

Billy picked up the bag. "Don't get too comfortable, you stupid bitch. I'll be around when you least expect it."

"Go to hell," she spat at him.

He'd already turned and started for his car.

Andi held her breath and her son, as the police, who'd been behind the trees, had quietly snuck around and surrounded Billy at his car.

"Police. Hands up and don't move," Andi heard one of them say.

"What the hell?" Billy, stupid man that he was, tried to run only to find himself tackled by one of the officers.

Crying, Andi focused on her son. She pulled him away from her, wanting to examine every inch of him. "How is my brave boy?" she asked. "Did he hurt you?"

"He pushed me around and grabbed me hard a couple of times. But I'm okay, Mom." His bright eyes shone with unshed tears.

"It's okay to cry," she told him, knowing he was trying to hold it in because he thought *she* was scared for him. "I cried when I found out he came and took you from Michael's house. And I'm crying now because I'm so happy I have you back."

His bottom lip quivered. "But you're a girl."

"And you're a brave boy. And brave men can cry and still be brave."

He sniffed and a tear fell from his eyes. She

wrapped him in her arms and let him have his moment.

Finally, they rose and together started toward the police officers, who had subdued and cuffed Billy. He was yelling at the officers and causing them trouble.

At the same time, another cruiser pulled up and her brother and Kyle jumped out of the car. Nicky took one look at his uncle and ran into his arms. Andi smiled at the two constant men in her life and breathed in deep.

"Andi."

She turned and Kyle pulled her into his embrace, his arms strong and comforting. "Jesus, I died twenty thousand times waiting for this to be over."

She clung to him. Because now that the time to be strong was over, she needed to fall apart and he was the only one she trusted to be there for her as she did. He held her as she cried tears of relief. He didn't judge her, he didn't do anything but be there. As he'd been there for her from the minute they'd reconnected.

He'd believed in her enough to let her handle Billy and for that she'd be eternally grateful. He'd proven himself to her in so many ways. He was everything she wanted… and, dammit, everything she deserved in a man. But before she could tell him how she felt, she had a past to put behind her.

She stepped out of his arms. "I need to do one

more thing," she told him.

Kyle looked into her eyes and nodded. "But I'm coming with you." He obviously understood what she needed to do.

She walked over to where Billy was cuffed and standing beside the police car. He was quieter than he'd been before, the seriousness of his circumstances obviously settling in.

When Andi discovered Billy had beaten his ex-girlfriend unconscious, leaving her bruised and bleeding on her apartment floor, she'd known how lucky she'd been to escape that fate.

"Can I have a minute?" she asked the officer.

"I have nothing to say to you," Billy said, belligerent and nasty as usual.

The officer nodded. "Go ahead. Before I put him in the car and take him away." He took two steps and turned away.

She met the gaze of the man who had tormented her for years and come back to do it again. Except this time she'd stood up to him. She'd held on to her family, her friends, and Kyle.

She straightened her shoulders. "You're a small little man," she told him. "You pick on people you think can't fight back. You're a bully and a bastard." She drew a deep breath. "I would say I wish I'd never met you, but you gave me one good thing in my life and that's Nicky. Other than my precious boy, I'm going to forget all about you, Billy. You're less than nothing to me."

"You stupid bitch. You think he won't get tired of you the way I did?"

She grasped Kyle's hand. "I know he won't," she said, head held high. "You'll be rotting in a jail cell and Kyle and I will live our lives. Together," she said, just to let him know that he didn't get his way.

Whatever he said next, she didn't listen. She turned her back on him and walked away. She only wished she'd had a chance to kick him in the balls before she'd left but with the police officer standing next to him, she'd refrained.

"We'll be in touch, Ms. Harmon," the officer said. "We'll need your statement and testimony if it goes to trial."

She nodded. "Whatever you need, I'll be available."

She walked over to Nicky and Kane, Kyle by her side, and together, she and her family headed home.

ANDI WORRIED ABOUT her son and the experience he'd had with his father. She had every intention of taking him to see a child psychologist because he needed to talk through what had happened to him and the fact that his own father could treat him the way he had. But she also knew her son was loved. He knew his mother would never leave him and always put his needs first. That had to count for something.

He'd fallen asleep but she couldn't help but check on him again. The light from the hallway illuminated the angry red marks on his arms and she closed her eyes, wishing she could have spared him the pain. She shut the door with a quiet click.

"Hey." Kyle came up behind her and put his arms around her waist. "Is he okay?" he asked quietly.

She nodded. "He's sleeping. I was just…"

"Watching him?" he asked knowingly.

She sighed. "Even knowing he's safe, it's hard to walk away."

Kyle stepped around her and opened Nicky's door wide enough that they'd hear him if he called out in his sleep or woke up and needed her. "Better?"

"Yes, thanks."

He took her hand. "Can we go into your room and unwind? Talk?"

"Of course." She wanted nothing more than to crawl into his arms. She had so much to say to him. So much to explain.

They walked down the hall and into her room. "Leave the door open so you can hear him," Kyle said.

She loved him for that alone.

They curled up together in her bed, Kyle's arms around her. "Can I talk first?" she asked.

"Could I stop you?"

She elbowed him in the stomach and laughed, appreciating him lightening the mood. But she immediately sobered, the events of the day... heck, the events of her *life* calling for a more serious conversation.

"I'm not sure where to begin," she said, pulling away from him so she could curl up on one side of the bed and meet his gaze.

"Wherever you're comfortable." He waited patiently, his handsome face set in a serious expression.

"I was young and stupid–" She held up a hand before he could argue with her. "Naïve. I was young and naïve. I didn't have a mother to look out for me and say, *Andi, you're making a mistake.* And I didn't trust in the one person who did tell me just that. I didn't believe in you and for that I'll always be sorry." She drew a deep breath. "But I meant what I said to Billy. I'll never regret Nicky."

Kyle's expression softened. "He's a great kid. Amazing, actually. And that's all because of you. He's the best of you, Andi. That's what he is."

She smiled, grateful he didn't look at her beloved boy and see his father. Hurdle one down, she thought.

"And then I compounded my mistakes by thinking

what Billy wanted me to think. That his abuse was my fault, that I deserved it. That I needed to hide it from the people who cared about me. And I really messed up when I cut you off and pushed you away. I should have believed you could handle yourself with Kyle, but I was so afraid, I couldn't see beyond my own fear. I hurt you and I know I didn't deserve a second chance at friendship, let alone the relationship we have now."

He shook his head. "You're wrong, Andi. Abusers succeed because they know just who to target. That doesn't make you wrong or bad or stupid or anything else you might think of yourself."

"I don't think that really. Not anymore. I say some of those things out of habit, but I know that I've worked hard to get past what happened. To be strong and independent – and that's where I made another mistake. I thought that I needed to go it alone."

He squeezed her hand, and she said, "You taught me that I don't have to. More than that, you taught me that I don't *want* to."

He smiled at her words. "Glad my teaching degree came in handy for something that means the world to me."

She laughed but her next words were serious. "I love you, Kyle. You're my best friend and you're the man I love. The only man I've ever really loved."

His golden-brown eyes softened. "That's good to

know. Because I love you, too. I always have. And to set the record straight, you're not the only one who makes mistakes. I should have told you how I felt years ago. Maybe I could have spared you—" He trailed off with a shake of his head.

"Nicky," they both said at the same time.

"If I'd told you I loved you sooner, if you'd wised up about Billy, you wouldn't have Nicky." He met her gaze. "*We* wouldn't have Nicky."

"I love you," she said again, her voice thick with emotion. Emotion she'd been afraid to feel until he'd come back into her life.

He lifted her chin, looking into her eyes. "I love you, too. And when the time is right, I want to marry you and make Nicky my son."

She blinked, her eyes opening wide.

He grinned, unrepentant for throwing that at her out of the blue. And she didn't care. Not one bit. She grinned back at him, happier than she'd ever been.

"Now kiss me," he said.

With a smile on her face, she leaned over and sealed her lips over his, knowing with everything in her that the dreams she'd had as a young girl, of falling in love, marrying a good man, and having the family she'd always wanted, had finally come true.

Epilogue

Summer

I *NOW PRONOUNCE you husband and wife.*

The words still rang in Kyle's ears as the celebration portion of his and Andi's wedding continued in the backyard of Halley and Kane's beach house. They'd opted for a small gathering of close friends and family, the people who meant the most to them.

Kyle had waited a lifetime for Andi, first because he'd been too shy to admit to his feelings and later because he'd waited too long and lost his chance. He'd had his life in Chicago, dated his share of women, but none had lived up to the memory of the girl who had his heart.

Now she was his. Her son was his.

Billy, difficult and narcissistic as usual, was fighting all the charges against him. The prosecutors were convinced he would end up with a longer sentence on the assault, kidnapping, and the host of other charges in both New York and Connecticut that were pending against him. Suffice it to say, the man would be going away for a long time.

Kyle and Andi had hired a lawyer who had no problem convincing Billy to sign away for good the parental rights he'd never wanted to begin with and the state of Connecticut had officially signed off on the termination because the man was a risk to his own son. Thus, the door had been opened for Kyle to adopt Nicky, which they'd done before getting married. He and Andi agreed, they wanted to be a family in every sense of the word.

Andi glided up to him, glowing in her white wedding gown and bare feet on the sand. As far as she was concerned, this was the marriage that counted and she'd wanted to do it right.

"Did you hear the news?" she asked, wrapping her arms around his neck.

He shook his head. "I don't think so. What's up?"

"Braden proposed to Juliette. They didn't want to take the spotlight off our wedding and they tried to keep it quiet, but she has a pretty sparkling ring on her finger that says it all. And I'm so happy for them!"

Clearly Andi didn't mind sharing that spotlight. He couldn't imagine that she would be anything but thrilled for the other couple.

"And they're talking about a destination wedding. Sounds heavenly." Her eyes glittered with happiness.

"As long as no one shows up on our honeymoon in Turks and Caicos, I'm good." He was happy to share most things, but not his island time with his wife.

In addition to waiting on the adoption to be legalized, they'd also waited until the summer to marry, when Kyle wouldn't be working, so they could take their honeymoon.

Kane and Halley had had a baby girl a few months ago, a beautiful baby who was loved and welcomed into the family with so much joy. Phoebe, meanwhile, was waddling around the beach at the wedding, hugely pregnant. So Kyle's mom would watch Nicky during the honeymoon and he couldn't wait to get his wife alone.

"Mom?"

Andi glanced at Nicky, wearing a mini version of Kyle's tuxedo… and bare feet.

"What's up?" she asked, although he had Halley's little black dog in his arms, which gave Kyle a clue.

"I was wondering… if when you got back from your honeymoon… could we get a dog? Please? I'll walk him and feed him. Please?" He looked up at her with big… puppy dog eyes.

"Umm… Kyle and I need to discuss it," she said.

Nicky turned that big-eyed gaze Kyle's way. "Dad?" he asked. "Can we get a dog?"

Dad.

Nicky had called him Dad for the first time.

At his words, the blood rushed from Kyle's head. He was so shocked, he was glad he still had one arm wrapped around Andi to hold him up and keep him from falling.

Just like that, the boy had gotten himself a dog, Kyle thought.

"We'll talk about it after the honeymoon," Andi said when Kyle was obviously too overcome to find words.

"You're going to get a friend," Nicky whispered to the dog in his arms as he walked away.

"He's pretty sure of himself," Andi said. She glanced at Kyle. "Are you okay, *Dad?*" she asked with a pleased grin.

"I'm better than I've ever been." He spun her around and dipped her, kissing her long and hard before letting her up for air. "I can't wait to get you alone, Mrs. Davenport." His dick hardened inside his pants, and he silently cursed that they had the rest of the reception to get through before he could truly make her his.

"And I'm looking forward to some of your dirty talking, Mr. Davenport."

"We have a lifetime of dirty talk and more to look forward to." He grasped her hand. "Now let's go celebrate with our family and friends."

Stay tuned for Carly's next super sexy read, **TAKE ME AGAIN** and read on for more information including an excerpt!

TAKE ME AGAIN

He's used to getting what he wants... but she's going to make him work for it.

Sebastian Knight is a closer. Be it a real estate deal or the woman of his choice, everything he wants is his for the taking.

Sexy and irresistible, a wink, a smile, or a handshake always seals the deal.

Until everything unravels around him.

After Ashley Easton's social climbing mother married into the Knight family, Ashley knew better than to get involved with sexy, trouble making Sebastian Knight but their attraction is undeniable, their chemistry intense, and in a moment of weakness, she turns to him, a mistake that cost her her home and her family. After she was sent away, she swore she'd never come back.

Sebastian never expected to see Ashley, the one woman he's never been able to get over, again.

When she walks back into his life at the worst possible time, more beautiful than ever, he's ready for a second chance. She's sassy and sexy everything he's ever desired. And she's back for good. Except Ashley wants nothing to do with the playboy who broke her heart. Too bad his sex appeal makes it harder and harder to keep him at arm's length.

Sebastian Knight might have a talent for sealing the deal but this is one game he's going to have to work to win.

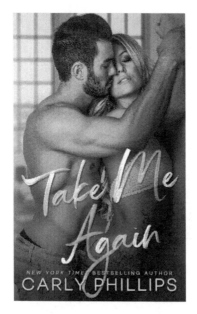

TAKE ME AGAIN

Please note: This is an unedited excerpt for your enjoyment.

Chapter One

S EBASTIAN KNIGHT'S HEAD pounded like a mother fucker and light streamed in from the window, piercing through one eye and into his brain. He groaned and rolled over, burying his face in the pillow. At twenty-six, wasn't he too damned old for a hangover like this? Yeah, he'd have to remember that the next time he picked up a glass of tequila and asked the bartender to keep them coming to celebrate closing a huge land deal with his brothers. Except Ethan and Parker had gone home after toasting their success. After that, Sebastian didn't remember much.

A flash of red flickered through his mind. A woman with flame-hued hair had joined him at the bar. He recalled the unusual color and the obviously fake but very tempting breasts that protruded over the top of her tight dress along with his body's reaction to her assets.

Shit.

Was he alone now?

He lifted his head and opened his eyes, not seeing anyone laying beside him and not recognizing where he was, but from the abundance of white furniture and the generic feel and look of the place, it was definitely a hotel room. An upscale suite but a hotel nevertheless.

Memory came back in small increments.

The huge parcel of land they'd bought, outbidding some major players because Sebastian had stepped in and closed the deal, something he excelled at and which his brothers counted on him to do.

He and his brothers choosing The Bar at the Baccarat Hotel in which to celebrate.

The toast and his first sip of Don Julio 1942 and how smooth it felt going down his throat.

And though he might not remember making the elevator ride up to this hotel room, he was here. Which meant *he'd* be the one making his escape from this one night stand, hopefully without too much of a scene.

The click of a door sounded and the redhead walked out of the bathroom, a towel wrapped around her body. Her cleavage was as ample as he remembered, her hair as red, her face? Not as pretty as he'd have hoped or as she'd probably appeared to his drunk self.

He scrubbed a hand over his gritty eyes and pushed up to a sitting position.

"Morning, lover." She started towards him, her stride confident, but he wasn't in the mood for small talk or sex.

Instead of waiting for her to ease onto the mattress alongside him, he slid out of bed and rose to his feet.

He glanced down to find his pants, grateful to see a torn condom package on the floor beside his clothes. Thank God, even in his inebriated state, he'd been smart about wrapping up.

"Aren't you going to stick around for a morning quickie?" she asked, as she opened the towel, revealing her naked body, his for the taking.

His dick didn't even perked up at the sight of her tits and he shook his head. "Sorry, doll," he said, because he didn't remember her name, dressing as he spoke. "I have a meeting I need to get to."

Her pout was real. "Didn't you have a good time last night?" she asked, sounding hurt, fumbling to cover herself with the towel again in the face of his rejection.

I don't remember wasn't what she wanted to hear.

He zipped his trousers and slid on his white dress shirt, buttoning up. "It was great. But now it's over," he said, knowing he had to be very clear about his intentions or lack thereof. Socks and shoes went on next and he was dressed and ready to go.

He patted his pockets, double checking for his wallet and cell phone and headed for the door. As awkward as this was, no need to prolong it or make it worse.

"Bastard," she muttered.

And after he'd pulled the door closed, he heard

what sounded like a shoe being thrown as the door clicked shut behind him. Yeah, he really was getting too old for this shit.

He pulled out his phone, only to discover he'd turned off the ringer sometime during the night and his brothers had tried to reach him numerous times. So had his younger sister, Sierra.

He narrowed his gaze. Why the hell had everyone been looking for him?

He took the elevator down to the first floor and walked through the lobby, across the white marble and out into the Manhattan sunshine before hitting redial and calling his oldest brother, Ethan. When the call went direct to voicemail, he dialed Parker next.

"Where the fuck have you been?" his middle sibling all but yelled.

"Calm yourself, Switzerland," he said, using the nickname the family had for Parker when he wouldn't take one side or another in an argument and always tended to remain neutral. "I'm here now. What's going on?"

Squinting into the sun, Sebastian hailed the first empty cab he saw, the driver coming to a skidding stop on his side of the street.

"Mandy died, Sebastian."

He froze, his hand on the taxi door handle. "Say that again."

"Mandy died," he said of Ethan's wife. "I've been with E. all night. So has Sierra. So get your ass to his place like yesterday."

The cab driver honked the horn, letting Sebastian know he'd better climb in in the back seat or the man would take off. He opened the door and slid onto the taped up pleather, his heart heavy and thudding inside his chest.

"What happened?" he asked through his thick throat and dry mouth.

Everyone loved Ethan's wife, Amanda, Mandy for short, who ran the accounting for Knight Associates, their land development/real estate firm.

"Buddy, where to?" the cab driver asked, impatiently.

He gave the address of the apartment building uptown that Knight Associates owned, where all the siblings resided.

Parker waited for Sebastian to finish before he answered. "Accidental overdose."

"What the fuck?" Mandy didn't take drugs, not that he knew of.

"It's a long story." Parker sounded exhausted. "Just come home and I'll explain everything."

"How's Ethan?" he asked, worried about his older brother who felt it was his job to look after everyone else.

He'd taken on the role of caretaker after their mother passed away when Sebastian had been fifteen. Only nineteen at the time, Ethan had stepped up because frankly, their father had never been the responsible parent.

"About as good as you'd expect," Parker muttered.

Which meant not good at all.

He needed to get to his sibling but the Manhattan traffic moved at a snail's pace and the ride seemed to take forever. He closed his eyes throughout the trip uptown and pictured Ethan's wife, a petite brunette with a vibrant personality. Granted, she'd been more subdued lately, her shoulder surgery last year having been hard on her physically and mentally. But an accidental overdose? It didn't compute.

The cab finally came to a stop. He shoved his credit card into the slot and completed the transaction, climbing out of the car and making his way past the doorman, into the building and up the elevator, another ride which seemed endless.

Arriving at Ethan's door, he knocked once and Sierra let him in, wrapping her arms around him, her smaller body shaking as she cried. The Knight siblings were each two years apart and he was close to his twenty-four year old baby sister. He walked into the apartment, Sierra holding onto him, and found his brothers in the living room.

She stepped away, sniffing as she sank into an oversized chair. From his place on the sofa, Ethan rose to his feet. His brother's dark hair was disheveled, his eyes bloodshot and red.

In silence, Sebastian stepped forward and pulled him into a brotherly embrace. "I'm sorry man," he said at last. "What happened?"

Ethan straightened to his full height. "I came home. Thought she was napping but I couldn't wake her up. I called 911 but it was too late." His voice sounded like gravel, the pain etched in his face raw and real.

"Parker–" Sebastian gestured to his brother who was now sitting on the far side of the couch. "Parker said it was an overdose but I don't understand. Over-dose on what?"

"Sit," Ethan said and Sebastian chose a matching chair next to Sierra's. "It was Oxy."

"What the fuck!?"

Ethan shook his head, obviously at a loss.

"It started after the shoulder surgery," Parker said, taking over when Ethan's voice failed him. "The doctors loaded her up with drugs to help with the pain. We had no idea they kept giving them to her until she was hooked."

Sebastian blinked in surprise, whether at Mandy's addiction he'd known nothing about or his middle brother's use of the word *we* when describing the situation, he couldn't be sure. The one thing Sebastian did know, he wasn't part of that *we*.

Before he could respond, Parker continued. "Remember the vacation she took with friends six months ago?" When Sebastian nodded, Parker said, "Rehab."

With everything Sebastian was learning, his head spun more. "Shit. I'm sorry." He ran a hand through his already disheveled hair.

"There's more," Parker said. He glanced at Ethan, who gave him a nod, obviously imparting permission to share the rest of the information.

Frozen, Sebastian waited. What more could there possibly be? Mandy's death wasn't enough?

Ethan rose and walked to the huge window overlooking the city, as Parker leaned forward. "In the last few months, as Mandy's addiction grew, she was skimming from the business to cover the cost of her pills."

"Jesus."

"Ethan tried to protect her, to get her into rehab, to replace the money… things spiraled. We'll be okay but you needed to know. Because the police are digging into where she got the pills. It could become public. Ugly."

As he began to put the pieces together of what his brother was telling him, Sebastian reeled with what, so far, had gone unsaid. "You aren't shocked by this and not because Ethan told you last night, after Mandy died." From the matter of fact way Parker had relayed the information, as if he'd already digested it and it had settled inside him, it was obvious. "You've known all along."

Parker merely nodded.

He glanced at his sister, who sat wide-eyed on the chair next to his. "What about you? Did you know?" he asked.

She swallowed hard. "Mandy told me recently that she was having problems. I talked to Ethan about it. I didn't know about the business issues until last night."

"So everyone knew something. But me." Sebastian rose to his feet, hurt and betrayal warring with anger, combining with grief inside him.

Parker met his gaze. "I was there the first time he found her pills. That's all."

But Sebastian sensed there was more to it. That he'd been left out of the loop for a reason. He glanced at Ethan.

"We didn't want to bother you with serious shit," Ethan said. "You didn't *need* to know. We were handling it."

"I didn't need to know or you didn't trust me to keep it to myself?" Sebastian asked, the truth crystallizing without his brother having to say anything. "Admit it. You were afraid I'd share info., like the Williamson deal."

It'd been his first year in the business and he'd been having a drink with a beautiful blonde. He didn't know at the time she was the daughter of the man against whom they were bidding for a piece of property. He was young, cocky and stupid. She was busty which distracted him, and extremely bright. He'd bragged they were sure to snag the property, that nobody would come close to their number. She hung on him, praised him, made him feel important and he'd admitted that they'd maxed out their bid. They couldn't go higher. It was all the information she'd needed to grab the property out from under them. Because of his big mouth.

Ethan blew out a harsh breath. "Fine, I didn't want it getting out that Mandy had a problem, okay? I figured the less people who knew, the better."

He straightened his shoulders and glared at his sibling. "Six fucking years and you can't let it go? You were handling it as a family and didn't think I needed to be part of it? I couldn't have helped? I couldn't have been there for you?" he asked, voice rising.

"Not with something this sensitive!" Ethan shot back.

Parker rose, stepped over to Sebastian and placed a hand on his shoulder. "Now's not the time," he told him.

Glancing at Ethan, his older brother's shoulders hunched, his pain obvious, Sebastian agreed. "He's right. You're hurting and you don't need to deal with this shit right now."

There'd be time for Sebastian's anger at his family later, after they'd all grieved for Mandy.

Want even more Carly books?
CARLY'S BOOKLIST by Series – visit:
http://smarturl.it/CarlyBooklist

Sign up for Carly's Newsletter:
http://smarturl.it/carlynews

Carly on Facebook:
facebook.com/CarlyPhillipsFanPage

Carly on Instagram:
instagram.com/carlyphillips

Rosewood Bay Series

Fearless

Breathe

Freed

Dream

About the Author

Carly Phillips is the *N.Y. Times* and *USA Today* Best-selling Author of over 50 sexy contemporary romance novels featuring hot men, strong women and the emotionally compelling stories her readers have come to expect and love. Carly's career spans over a decade and a half with various New York publishing houses, and she is now an Indie author who runs her own business and loves every exciting minute of her publishing journey. Carly is happily married to her college sweetheart, the mother of two nearly adult daughters and three crazy dogs (two wheaten terriers and one mutant Havanese) who star on her Facebook Fan Page and website. Carly loves social media and is always around to interact with her readers.

Made in the USA
San Bernardino, CA
30 January 2019